HOUSE OF OTTER 3

Saving
ALEXANDER

HOUSE OF OTTER 3

Saving
ALEXANDER

LEO SPARX

4 Horsemen
Publications, Inc.

Dedication

To my readers
for being otter worldly.

QUEER ZOOLOGY

Otter (n): *a man who is leaner than a cub or bear but still covered in fur*

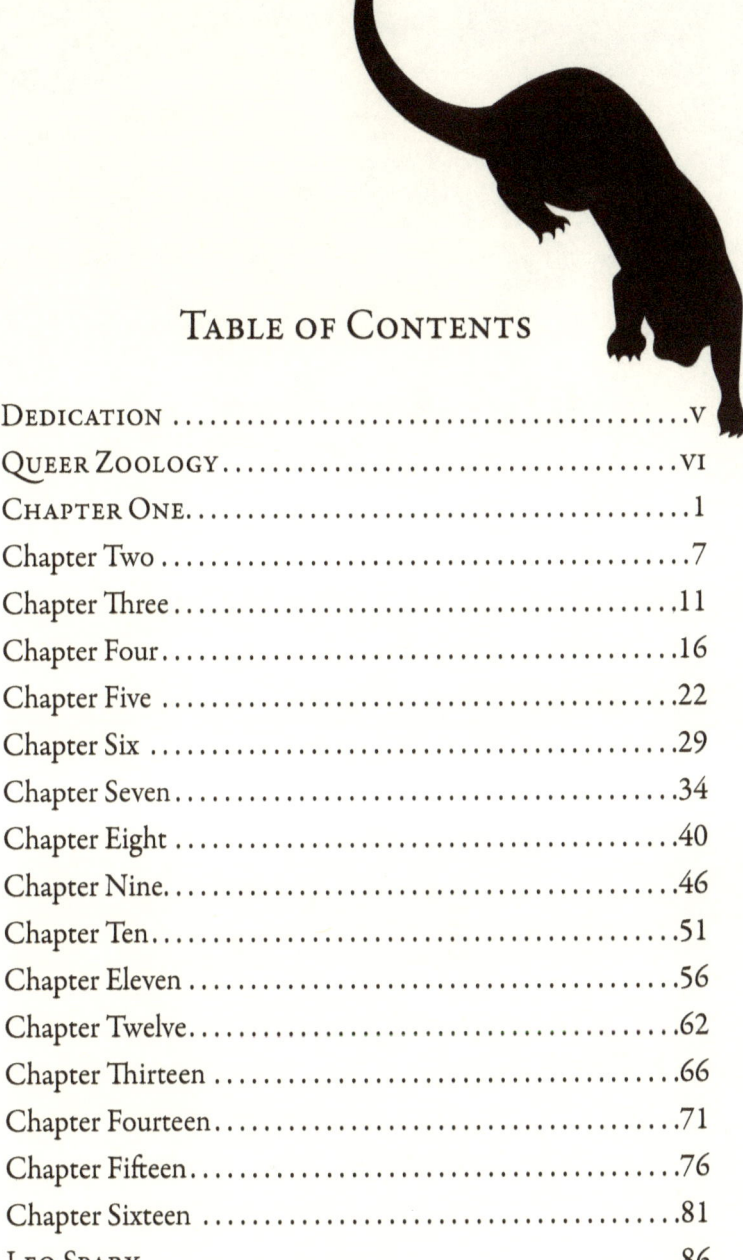

Table of Contents

CHAPTER ONE

C haos.

Chaos is what you get when seven men occupy any house, no matter the size. When they sat around the long banquet table during the day, it was easier to see the marks on arms and shoulders: the shape of the same hand, dark across nearly every shade of face. On any part without a beard or mustache or fur, there was some lasting sign of discipline.

But today the thing on everyone's mind was food. It was whatever Darius had cooked up in the kitchen that smelled so good. Usher was on a trip for the first time in weeks. With just me and the boys in the house, it was home, but in a much larger floor plan.

"If we're gonna do it, then we're gonna do it right," Darius said as the door from the kitchen swung open and settled back into place. He was wearing his apron, and not unlike the small quarters we used to call a house, everyone was as close to naked as possible.

Darius set a large dish in the center of the table where we'd all gathered at the middle seats. Taking off the apron, he settled into an empty chair and let the plushness of the seat cradle his ass.

Sonny was perched nearby, literally up on his bare feet more than sitting. With his knees bent, he hovered over the table setting identical to the one in front of each of us. He gripped an oversized fork and spoon that were definitely intended to be serving utensils. As they glimmered in the afternoon sun next to his nipple rings, I wondered what it was about gay men that made it impossible for us to sit correctly.

Neither Brent nor Marco's feet were flat on the floor either. Both of the blondes had dark roots growing from their scalp now. One draped his legs over the arm of the velvet dining room chair, and the other was on his knees. When one switched positions, the other followed. It had been like this for days. All of us sat just lazily eating and lounging in the various unlocked rooms of the house while its owner was away.

Something had changed after the boys arrived. Bedroom doors that would typically be locked were suddenly wide open. But as fun as it all felt, I knew well enough the freedom we were being allowed paired with a steep payment. Maybe not a bruise or sting, but something worse. A strange emptiness sat in my stomach, and it wasn't hunger. While the boys shoveled hot food into their mouths, the feeling loomed in the mansion like a ghost story I hadn't heard yet.

"Let's swim after lunch," Marco said, plopping something with gravy and vegetables on his plate. Darius shot me an *oops* look from across the table. I hadn't told anyone else about the pool, but apparently they all knew now.

Telling Darius the truth about Roderick being in the house hadn't been an easy conversation, but I didn't have an option after they'd seen each other. Even if their introduction had been less than informal, Darius seemed to know exactly who Roderick was while he knelt on the floor near him.

That night when Darius encountered the man he'd only heard stories about around town, I stood on the other side of the two-way glass. Looking at the collection of hairy men inside the dungeon, lights flashed on the control board and reflected in the window.

Just beyond it, I could see Roderick's cock dripping through the cage that had been put around him. The silver tray he braced on his flat hand held three whips ready for Usher to use at any time. They didn't seem heavy, but I could tell from the way Roderick's bent arm shook near the elbow that he had been suspending them for quite a duration.

He was being punished, and I should have been grateful that the blame was on him instead of me for our pool encounter. After all, he had lied to me. I'd scrubbed the house clean inside and out as penance for believing him, but this punishment was more severe. Observing his confinement, the way his cock and balls were secured behind the metal rungs of the cage, I wanted to feel vindicated.

I wanted to be angry at him.

But among the emotions I felt observing my former house-mates knelt on the cement and Roderick in agony, anger wasn't one of them. Usher had noticed me, even if I wasn't certain how he'd spotted my form through the glass. No one else had. Perhaps they were too focused on the hurt about to be inflicted upon their bodies.

With a wink in my direction, the man in the suit, the only one wearing real clothing, grabbed the smallest whip from the silver tray. Roderick's arm trembled, and he straightened his legs. Small droplets drizzled from him until they hit the floor.

Usher smirked and stuck a single finger through the rungs of the cage. He ran his thumb over the moisture and rubbed it along the length of the skin he could access beyond the barrier. My former partner-in-crime winced, knowing the harder he got, the more the cage would push back against him. It looked like Usher laughed, but I couldn't hear him.

I glanced at the buttons and dials on the control board. A lever with an ear symbol and ascending bars seemed a strong possibility to add audio to the movie playing out in front of me. Unsure if I should risk it, I moved the tab slowly upward, expecting to accidentally turn on some sort of music or completely cut the lights. An intrusive thought crossed my mind: I could ruin Usher's façade, abruptly fading his scene to black. It was almost funny, but I knew the swift punishment that would follow would not hold the same humor. Right now, for whatever reason, he was sparing me from participating in the ceremony, but he could have me on the other side of that glass whenever he wanted.

Luckily, the lever I'd chosen seemed to open a channel, and now I could hear the whimpers coming from the boys. They posed with mouths open, tongues out, the whip tapping at their inner thighs. When Usher's spit landed inside each of them, they held it there until he commanded them to swallow. I watched the bulge of his DNA travel through their throats. If it hadn't been official before, it was now.

Usher looked up toward me again and smirked. Turning away from the four vulnerable hairy men, he stood in front of Roderick and his caged cock. He set the whip he'd been using on the tray and exchanged it for one resembling a riding crop. Roderick didn't move his face, but his eyes stared down at Usher's selection. I'd forgotten how long his eyelashes were, the way they could make his eyes glitter when he experienced extreme emotion: happiness, sadness, horniness, fear.

With a few slaps on Usher's palm, the riding crop cracked, echoing through the concrete room. The boys behind him seemed to tremble, but for just a second, I thought I saw Sonny smile. I shook my head, assuming the last thing Usher would want is for a boy to be amused by his sadism.

Using his shiny shoe, Usher pushed at Roderick's bare foot just below the ankle. "Wider," he said. Roderick obeyed immediately and another drizzle found its way through the cage and to the floor below. With his thighs farther apart, Roderick's balls were exposed and available to Usher. The suited man used his grip on the riding crop to issue quick controlled movements, three taps in a row to Roderick's sensitive hanging skin.

It looked like his knees may buckle until Usher said, "You had better not drop my tray, boy." Roderick steadied himself, and a tear fell from his eye in rhythm with new droplets of precum from his cock. Behind Usher, Sonny bit his lip to stifle another smile, and Darius moved his body close enough to jab him with his elbow. He looked at him with wide eyes as if to say *stop*.

Darius had seen more than the other three boys in this house and learned quickly the extent of Usher's playtime. I still had yet to experience the sounding rods he had told me about, but I saw them shining from a rack, fully sanitized and prepared. Since Usher had developed a fascination with inserting the long metal dowels into Darius specifically, the last thing he needed was for Sonny to invite punishment with a little giggle.

Maybe he was nervous or maybe still stoned from the outside world—I still had no idea how long they had been here before the ritual began—but whatever the reason, Sonny couldn't stop his glee about being in bondage. Usher must have heard the interaction because he spun around quickly, catching Sonny mid-smirk. The long-haired man let the expression dissolve from his face the moment the man holding the whip had his eyes on him, but the damage had already been done.

Leaving Roderick standing in place, still balancing the tray and in visible pain, Usher focused on Sonny. He walked slowly toward the line of boys and stopped at the end, letting the surfer's face fall directly in front of the closed zipper of his slacks.

"Look at me, boy," Usher said and grabbed Sonny roughly by the trimmed beard on his chin.

"Are you having fun?" Usher asked when Sonny's eyes turned upward. Sonny looked at him almost fearlessly, but just next to him, Darius inhaled deeply, bracing himself for whatever was to come. Sonny didn't answer, and a strange silence hung in the air while all focus was on the interaction.

Unexpectedly, Usher began stroking Sonny's long hair and tucked a lock behind his ear. When it was in place, the suited man pulled his hand away and smiled, wide. Sonny's body relaxed. Then, more rapidly than a lightning strike, Usher cracked his open palm across Sonny's face. He grabbed a handful of his luscious locks and said, "You'll be first, boy."

CHAPTER TWO

"The word of the day is Voyeurism, boys." Usher paced between the weight bench and the suspended sling fastened to the ceiling with chains. There always seemed to be something new in the red room no matter how many times I was in it. The sling with the stain-resistant canvas hanging from eyelets by four points was the latest addition.

Usher tapped a new whip on the outside of his leg. Not far from the bench Usher had fucked me on before, Sonny was balled on the floor, still reeling from the impact on his stubbly cheek. Closer to the swaying sling, Roderick's forearm shook under the platter full of toys, and he gritted his teeth, determined to keep it level.

When Usher wrapped his hand around one of the linked metal ropes, I wondered what it would be like to be cradled then pushed and pulled by him in the hammock. He had probably only added the new apparatus to gain easier access for inserting toys into holes, but even considering the possibility of his cock sliding in and out of me using the sling's rhythm was getting me hard.

"Do you like being watched, boy?" Usher's shiny loafers clicked across the spotty cement until he reached the other side of the line where Marco sat like a statue in his collar. Not far from him, just past Marco's brother, Darius fought to stay in position, his eyes on Sonny, who was still on the floor.

"Perhaps with your twin?" Usher said, abandoning his flogging tool with a clatter to the floor to free his hands and stroke each of the brother's fuzzy chests. He pinched a nipple on each then perched himself in front of them. Lowering his body, he traced a finger down their stomachs, stopping just before the thick bands of their matching jockstraps. I couldn't help but stare at his ass in those tight linen pants as he hovered just above the ground.

Brent and Marco squealed in unison under his touch. When Usher rose to a standing position again, retrieving the whip in the process, they both flinched and drew their faces back. The synced movement seemed to please Usher—as if some balance had been restored.

He grabbed the chain connecting the four men's collars— the way Roderick and I had been connected—and followed the links until he could tug on the line leading directly to Sonny. "Up, boy," he growled, apparently done with Sonny's dramatic display of anguish from the single open-handed strike.

"Does it arouse you knowing that someone is seeing you submit to me?" Usher spoke to the room, in no particular direction, while Sonny wiggled to his feet and tossed his long hair back in place behind his shoulders. With his cat-like friend back on his knees, Darius leaned his body into Sonny's side as if to ask if he was alright or reassure him in some way. I looked at Usher, who luckily hadn't caught the tender moment with his back turned.

"Do you feel it, boys? His eyes on you now?" Usher turned toward the window, toward me. It had taken me until that moment and his eyes piercing through the mirror to realize he was talking about me in his monologue.

My breath became quick and shallow. I worried I'd opened more than a one-way channel when I'd been searching for the room's soundtrack. Maybe the entire time, he'd heard me breathing. Maybe they all knew I was watching.

"This type of voyeur gets just as much excitement out of seeing domination as they do being dominated. Possibly more." He wasn't telling the boys anything they didn't know. As professionals, we'd all been paid to have an audience before, but that wasn't the point he was making. His words weren't for the men in the room; they were for me. My cock dripped and pooled precum in the thin cotton of my white briefs while he talked.

"Someone is getting hard," he said, still focused on the two-way mirror. Reaching down to his slacks, he rubbed over his zipper. The bulge of his thickness was unmistakable, and with all the men only having a view of his back, he stroked through his dress pants. No one else could see from their position behind him when he pulled his zipper down and reached his hand into the depths. The display was for me alone.

A brief moment of pleasure overtook his face while he gazed through the window that wasn't intended to be transparent. Our eyes locked, but I still wasn't certain if I was actually visible. I was afraid to breathe, but following his hand rubbing up and down on his hardness, a trembling sigh escaped my mouth. My cock pulsed.

His expression changed abruptly, and he pulled the zipper back up in a single motion. Usher cleared his throat and turned on his heels, dropping his arms to his sides. "Take them to their rooms. We're done now." His words were directed at Roderick, who seemed both surprised and skeptical.

Nervously, he attempted to bend and set the tray on the cement, but it slipped. Solid metal and rubber-wrapped tools bounced against the indoor pavement. Roderick froze in humiliation and embarrassment with his swollen balls between his legs.

Usher closed his eyes and shook his head but didn't turn to acknowledge the crash. "Go now!" he yelled. Roderick gathered the whips and set them back on the silver platter quickly before motioning for the tied boys to stand. They followed him from the room like a strange BDSM Pride parade, and the door slid closed behind them.

When the room was clear, Usher stood in the dim light and wiped his hands clean. The gesture seemed ritualistic as I'd seen him do it before, almost as an indication of completion

He looked up to the panel again. "Did you enjoy the show, boy?" he asked, tracing his reset hands over the whips he hadn't used. "I did have to cut it a little short."

I was uncertain whether or not he could hear me, but that wasn't the only reason I didn't respond. There was a chance, I thought, maybe, if I stayed quiet enough, I could avoid being punished for disturbing the ritual. When I was involved, it had seemed so important to him.

So much of me wanted to transport myself through the window. It had been too long since he'd touched me, and I'd been trying so hard to get his attention during my punishment. But he had an all too familiar twinkle in his eye, like a wild animal poised to tear me to shreds.

"Come inside, boy," he said and tapped on the glass like a fish tank. Even on the side of the predator, in this control room, I was still his prey. Knowing that made me so hard my cock pushed at the cotton of the white briefs. On the other side of the barrier, Usher rubbed his hand over the growing bulge under his slacks and said, "Don't keep me waiting."

CHAPTER THREE

The path from the control room to the dungeon wasn't straightforward. It seemed odd to me that while they were connected by the pane of glass, they felt miles apart when I walked with my boner across the tile floor and down the hallway. When I opened the door, he was standing there, still prepared to pounce but with a strange smirk on his face.

"Down," he said, not wasting any time. Immediately, the chill of the cement was on my kneecaps. I could have opened my mouth to say sorry for accidentally disobeying him or to tell him I understood why I had been punished. I could have told him how much I'd missed him. But he was already taking out his cock for me, and all I wanted, more than telling him how I felt, was to have his dick in my mouth.

"Did you wear those for me, boy?" he asked, rubbing the warm tip of his girth against my closed lips. I couldn't remember if there had been precum when I'd had the opportunity to taste him before, but tonight he was spreading it over the soft skin on the outside of my mouth.

"I do remember them," he said, parting my lips with his fingers and pushing the taste of him to my tongue, "but it wasn't what you were wearing the first night I saw you."

With two fingers in my mouth now and thrusting them in and out, I couldn't have spoken even if I'd wanted to. He had told me before that he knew he wanted me back when he'd watched me jerk-off in the woods outside the house. But, to me, the first night we met was when I'd heard his voice on the computer. In a time that seemed centuries away now—when he was a black screen and nothing more.

That was before he'd become the object of so much of my affection, before the need to have him in my life had gotten so strong. Before I knew, to gain a place in his world, I would trade anything: my skin, my freedom, my sex.

"What was it that brought you to me?" Usher asked, lifting my chin with a light touch so he could see into my eyes. He'd moved his fingers from my mouth so I could answer. A mix of my spit and his precum stuck to his fingertips, and he rubbed them together. Even with my mouth free, I didn't have the words to answer his question.

Roderick had been the one to orchestrate everything that brought me into the mansion. He arranged the false pretense to make me think being here would be something other than it was. If there was more Usher expected me to know, I didn't.

"It was the house," Usher said, turning his gaze to the room around us. "The house gave you to me." He stroked my hair and ran his hand down the side of my face. The suited man suddenly seemed sad and turned away. Walking toward the whips that remained within reach, he took a deep breath as he prepared to speak. While I waited to see if he would return his taste to me, I stayed silent.

"It drew you here and you told it yes. You consented to everything that has been done to you. Every ounce of pain and pleasure, you told the house you wanted it when you kept coming back. Every time you spilled your load to the dirt, you told the house to take you. That you belonged to it."

Usher approached with a whip that looked more like a thin fly swatter. It had holes like a wiffle ball or cheese grater for less resistance and, I assumed, harder hits.

"I need you to say two things," Usher said, twirling the loop of the swatter around his finger in a spiral motion. "First, tell me you're sorry for letting someone else touch you. Then tell me yes. Not to the house, but to me. Tell me you want all of this. Tell me that you want me."

Inhaling deeply, I didn't feel scared of the whip when I answered without hesitation, "Yes, I only want you." At first, I wasn't sure if the single sentence gave him the satisfaction he was after. But then his eyes were back on me, and he knelt directly in front of where I remained on the concrete.

He loosened his tie and brought my hands to his shirt buttons. I quickly pulled at them until his chest was exposed and, without permission, ran my hand through his dark fur. He didn't stop me.

My fingers rolled around his nipples, and he threw his head back before bringing it in close to my cheek. Usher moaned in my ear and whispered, "That feels incredible."

When he pulled back again, his stubble rubbed on mine and his lips lingered near my mouth. I thought he was going to kiss me, but he didn't. He was still taller than I was, but our height difference seemed less important when we were kneeling together. Turning my head, I let my lips hover near his but stopped myself from moving forward. My cock pulsed again as I imagined what our tongues would taste like wrapped together.

I thought the moment was over when he stood up, but instead, he took his dick out and motioned for me to open my mouth. Wrapping his hands around my head, he guided my wet lips until he could thrust himself deep into my throat.

With him fucking my face, I kept my eyes on him but rubbed over the white underwear. His precum dripped farther into me every time my lips met his pubic bone. Usher moaned again and said, "You never fail to impress me." He must have noticed me teasing my hardness because he nodded his head. "Go ahead."

Deep-throating the length of him, I concentrated on breathing through my nose so I wouldn't have to take a break from sucking him. His approval sent colorful butterflies through every part of me, but especially my balls, which were full and throbbing in step with my cock while I pumped and rubbed the tip.

His fingers wrapped in my hair, he pulled and pushed until he twitched in the tunnel of my tight throat. He was ready to burst. When I felt his warm cum explode and slide down toward my stomach, I stroked fast enough to erupt a full load to the hard floor below.

"I want to show you something," Usher said. I watched his cock grow soft. I couldn't believe he was still in the room after using my throat. His warmth was inside me, and yet, he was here.

He grabbed my hand and pulled me gently to my feet, then led me to an area just off the side of where the mirror was set into the wall. A rack of toys I'd polished only a day before hung in front of us.

If he was ready to pick one out to put inside of me or beat me with, my body wasn't prepared. I wanted to relax and breathe an adequate amount of oxygen for a minute.

Not that I was complaining.

Usher lifted the bottom of the pegboard, letting it rest on the two holding hooks above. Underneath was a button, not unlike the one he'd showed me the first night in the house, the same night I'd learned the meaning of the word *credenza*.

When he pushed the shiny button, the wall holding the rack developed lines on either side and above. Something made a popping sound like a spring had been holding it back. "Push, boy," Usher said, motioning to the wall. When I did as I was told, the wall became a door. On the other side was a room I'd seen once before. The one with the portraits of men.

"Short cut, for next time," Usher said, pulling the door closed again like a safe. He didn't seem to like being in the portrait room longer than necessary. I had many questions about why so many beautiful pieces of art were tucked away in a room no one ever saw when so much more of the art was prominently displayed around the house. But I was concentrating on the new secret door I'd been shown and thinking how helpful it would have been to know it was there before stumbling around the house with a hard on in my underwear. More than both those thoughts, I was most aware of him turning his body away from me once the pegboard lowered again and how badly I wanted him to stay.

"Good night, Alexander," he said as he left me behind in the dark room. It was a feeling that wasn't entirely new, but alone again, this time I was smiling. He had said my name. It was the first time he'd called me anything other than "boy."

CHAPTER FOUR

fter that night, I floated on clouds through the mansion. Every door seemed open to me, every passage no longer felt like a mystery. When I thought about a certain type of music, without fail, it seemed to play over the speakers.

Yet, I hadn't seen anyone—the boys, Roderick, even Usher—for days. If I had, I wasn't certain what I would say to any of them. My former best friend had gotten me in the kind of trouble that led to manual labor. For that, I knew I would never forgive him, even if his punishment of chastity for our encounter was worse than anything I'd endured.

My bliss and solitude led me to wonder: had it not been for Roderick bringing me out that night and showing me the control room, would Usher have longed for me enough to end his ritual and speak my name? Something had shifted in the energy of the house since our most recent exchange. But while I shook my hips and ass through the hallways, part of me worried the other boys weren't having nearly as much fun.

No matter where I wandered in the estate, I knew better than to go looking for anyone directly. Making so much progress with Usher meant continuing to respect his rules and his process, even if I didn't understand it. Whenever we did get a chance to be intimate again, I would ask him the questions I had been too overwhelmed to ask. At least he seemed more ready to offer me answers, and I finally felt prepared to hear them.

I thought an opportunity for a real conversation would present itself sooner rather than later until I woke up late one afternoon to a note on a tray outside my door. *How nostalgic,* I thought, as I opened the folded paper.

> *We will return shortly, boy.*
> *Make sure they behave.*

So, I was "boy" again, but I assumed that meant him using my real name was intended to be something private and shared only between us. It still felt special that way, and I was content believing it for now. But who was "*we*"?

Wherever he was going, this time, a phone hadn't been left for me. Having the device had felt like a privilege when it was awarded before, but seeing only the note gave me a sense of relief this time around. The constant messages and instruction were no longer necessary. He trusted me to take care of the house and everyone inside without monitoring and dictating my every movement.

No sooner had I set the note down then a body came flying through my door and landed on my unmade bed, "Oh girl! We have been released!" It was Darius, back in his favorite designer underwear on his thick ass. He seemed much happier than the last time we'd seen each other.

"I thought you were leaving," I said, collapsing back-first on the bed next to him.

"Girl, I was walking; I remember that much. Then I woke up back in my room."

"Yeah, that happens."

"You know, I'm not even mad about it though," Darius grabbed at one of my pillows and fluffed it. He examined the softness as if he were sizing it up against his own provided bedding, shopping. "Like, I spend all this time trying to get money, and here's this situation where it's just being handed to me. I'm gonna say no?"

He set my pillow behind his head to give it a test drive but immediately moved it and squinted. Displeased with its comfort, he set it back against the headboard. In a quick motion, he bounced off my bed and to his feet. "Anyway, I'm back, bitch!" Darius fell forward from where he stood between my legs and piled his bare chest on top of mine.

A familiar voice yelled some mumbled surfer-lingo happily from the hallway, then the weight of another male body was on me. I could see just the glint of Sonny's eye and some of his wavy hair from the bottom of the sandwich we'd created around Darius.

Two additional voices whooped and screamed until more naked chests were on either side of me. Smothered in chest and stomach hair from all angles, the dog pile of fur cocooned me in certainty I didn't know I needed. They weren't mad. They were okay. And while I knew I wouldn't have all the answers to whatever questions they needed to ask, while we were all out and free, I wanted to make sure they had a great time.

Days later, after our huge lunch, I guided the boys through the halls with towels over our shoulders. As we walked, I couldn't pinpoint exactly why I'd felt the need to keep the pool a secret. It wasn't Darius's fault he had told the other boys about it. The location wasn't sacred just because Roderick and I had fucked there.

It had felt magical that night, and part of me wondered if seeing it in the daylight and having the brothers doing cannonballs into the pristine water would taint it. But the house wasn't mine. If this was going to be our home, then it belonged to all of us.

At least until Usher returned.

The expensive flip-flops we'd each pulled from our closets squeaked against the tile as I tried to remember the path to the indoor pool. With the other boys trailing behind, Darius walked next to me. "I'm sorry I told them, but I'm just gonna say it: If he never comes back, you'll be better off," he said.

I didn't respond while I backtracked our group down a hallway lined with statues of men in singlets, their pebbled hair tufted in marble. "I told you before he was a bad news gay."

"Hot though," Marco said, peeking his bleached tips between us before moving back to a pedestal to stroke the elbow of one of the picturesque carvings.

"Even with clothes on," Brent said, circling the chiseled nipple near his brother's exploration. "He looked cute the other morning before he left."

I seemed to miss so many things when I allowed myself to sleep in, but it didn't take too long to string the details together. That was what the note had meant by "*we*." Usher had taken Roderick with him on his trip.

The clouds I'd been bouncing on dissolved from under me. Both men missing from the room had a unique ability to make me feel so special and then immediately blindside me with betrayal. They could do this separately just fine, but as a team, they had successfully ripped my heart into pieces. If Usher had brought Roderick instead of me, it meant he was his favorite.

Not me.

"Are we lost?" Sonny asked, leaning against a pillar. I hadn't realized we'd been walking in a circle and had stopped at a dead end.

Admittedly, I was distracted with the new information, but more so, the house seemed to have changed around me again.

The path I'd remembered to relocate the atrium wasn't the same, and instead of the decorative doors leading to the pool deck, the five of us stood at a full bookcase.

Our sandals sinking into the lush carpet, I was able to manage, "Sorry guys," before plopping down with defeat in a tufted chair. Resting my elbows on the polished handles and my head in my hands, I didn't mean to pout, but soon Darius had his arm around my shoulders. He balanced his weight against the furniture and circled his fingertips across my naked back.

"Which one are you sad about?" Darius asked. I knew he was posing the question because he wanted to help, even if it sounded like a read. We hadn't discussed everything during the short moments we'd had alone in the kitchen while he cooked, but he knew enough to understand the extravagance wasn't my only reason for staying in the house.

I'd learned a lot about the feelings I was capable of having for another man since living in the mansion, not all of them sexual. But as much information as I'd taken in since the last time I'd had a sad walk on the better side of town, I still had no idea how to answer Darius's question.

The other boys kept their distance, exploring the room that was new to all of us. It seemed to be a study or den considering the number of books.

Brent pulled a thick black-spined novel from the shelf and thumbed through it. I could hear him rustling the pages and showing them to his brother and Sonny.

"Wow, who are these guys?" Marco asked in my direction, pointing at the contents. They brought the book over to show me endless sketches of men in harnesses and jockstraps, tight jeans, and knee high socks. In thick lines, some had on leather and some latex. There were masks and hoods and gags and blindfolds. But through the hundreds of pages, they were all just as furry as the real boys standing in the room around me.

"Every book is like this," Brent said, pulling out more volumes and licking his finger to flip through them. The bookcase reminded me of the secret passage that led to the kitchen. I'd been told at the time which of the books to remove via text from Usher when I needed the information to move unseen through the mansion, but I'd never taken the time to browse through the other books. I'd assumed they were more sad literature. I was wrong.

No artist was credited to identify who had drawn the men. Nor were the provocatively posed models inside named. I did know there had been a letter on the outside of the book which opened to the kitchen passage.

"Is there a book with a P on it?" I asked Brent as he stood with a stacked armful of the pornographic encyclopedias.

He bent down and scanned through the selection then pulled one book out slowly. The large case slid with just the slightest tilt of the masked lever. Behind it was the massive atrium. The carpeted room had felt so solid and landlocked, now the expansive area in front of us made our surroundings echo.

The boys smiled and laughed, grabbing up their towels and running straight into the still pool. They dove and splashed while the tile mosaics lining the pool floor shimmered in the sun. Somehow, the water was even more beautiful than it had been under the moonlight.

Chapter Five

From my spot on the white lounge chair, I could see boys that had been whimpering with their hands behind their back no more than a few nights before—playing naked. With the sunlight illuminating each ripple in the reflective surface, the art above and below them held the luminescence in blue hues, making the water even more inviting.

Lifting a half-empty bottle of wine from the collection we'd hauled from the kitchen to my lips, I saw the nudity of an approaching man fisheye in the curve of a green glass.

"Come in!" Darius said before setting himself down on a long reclined chair next to me. I shook my head but smiled while he ran his hands through his moist hair. For a moment, I looked at his lips and thought about the night we'd said goodbye, the kiss we'd shared. I wondered if we'd ever mess around again living under this roof.

If I'd ever kiss any man at all.

Turning my eyes back to the bottle, I was basking in a buzz from room temperature red wine. It would have been nice to play with everyone, but thoughts about Usher and Roderick cycled endlessly through my brain. Being this close to a place so tied to deception only made me ask more questions.

In the pool, Sonny hoisted himself on his hands to the deck where another bottle of wine rested. His slightly muscular surfer arms flexed holding up his weight. The fur on his round ass clung with beads of pool water which, as he drank, ran down both cheeks and down his thighs. I looked at Darius, and he pursed his lips.

"Don't," I said, handing him the vessel of wine I'd been holding, hoping to sway his attention. "Whatever you're thinking, don't do it."

"Oh, is it an official rule?" Darius asked, swigging the burgundy back quickly. He wiped his mouth around the corners and smirked, knowing he wasn't asking a real question as much as commenting on the uncertainty of the entire situation. "All the men in this house and we're what, supposed to just take the pain and—"

"You didn't have to come back," I hadn't meant to cut him off. The alcohol and general anxiety made me irritable.

"I told you I woke up here after I left."

"Haven't heard you behind my wardrobe lately. You know he's gone now. You could try again." *I finally have friends here. Why am I being so bitchy?*

Darius popped his tongue. "Any chance you've got a point, girl?"

"All I'm saying is: he'll know. Whatever you do, he'll see it." With the bottle back in my hand, I sucked on the hole at the top. I let too much liquid bitterness enter my mouth before I winced and swallowed with one gulp.

He watched me drink as we sat in a moment of brief silence. Maybe Darius didn't want to spoil the afternoon, but instead of copying my tone, he shifted his tactic and smirked. "Is that why you're still wearing this bathing suit?" he asked, running his hand near my waistband.

I pushed his hand away. Defeated, he rose suddenly and stood in front of my chair. Scanning the area, he put his arms in the air. "I don't see any cameras in here."

Just behind Darius, Marco and Brent took turns sitting on each other's shoulders and walking into the deep end until the one on top was underwater. Sonny was balanced on his elbows, half in, half out of the water like a merman. He smiled when Darius turned to meet his eye.

Looking back at me, he said, "Try to have some fun while you can, girl. I know I'm gonna," then turned fully toward the water and dove in.

I followed his bubbles popping on the surface of the pool until he reached where Sonny presented himself. Darius pulled him playfully into the water, and the two naked men kissed and tussled among the waves. The brothers stopped their game when Darius set Sonny on the steps and put his head between the merman's legs to lick and suck.

Sonny moaned, and I gulped on the bottle. I wasn't certain if I was jealous or just aware that their every action would somehow be blamed on me.

Every day went like this for a week: waking up late hungover, eating something, going to the pool, getting fucked up all night, only to do it again the next day. There hadn't been a word from Usher—no notes or messages. Glass bottles lined the hallways and dishes stacked up in the kitchen. The house was a disaster.

Like everything else, I assumed we were intended to be the housekeepers, but no roles had been assigned by Usher. No instructions had been left other than for me to keep them in check, but as the days and sips blended together, I gave up reminding them to clean up after themselves. I gave into letting them believe they had found the only room in the house without surveillance. There were many things that could be called punishment in the house, but it seemed they would need to learn that on their own.

When I felt myself passing out on the lounge chair, my eyes were closing to a scene of the four men on each other's shoulders: Brent on Sonny and Darius on Marco, their dicks, balls, and wet hair all rubbing together as they laughed. Forearms slapped moist skin, chests against open palms, until one duo pulled the other down into the water, and they started over again.

Their joyous yells became white noise among the clicking bottles bobbing in the sparkling pool until I awoke to intense moaning. My eyes parted slowly, revealing motion unfolding only a few feet away. Next to me on the closest lounger was Darius, his head between Sonny's legs again.

With Sonny's fingers wrapped in Darius's hair, Sonny grabbed his head and guided his mouth back and forth on his cock. Sonny thrust his hips forward to fuck Darius's mouth and growled with pleasure. Darius pulled back from the grip only to lick the precum from his lips then dove back in to devour Sonny whole, gliding his tongue across every part of him.

Behind them, Brent and Marco sat on another fully-reclined lounge chair. Their hairy knees touched while they stroked their cocks. Below the weight of their furry asses, the stretchy plastic straps lengthened and their balls hung full near the metal piping supporting the chair. In predictable unison, the brothers spit into their hands and brought the lubricant to their shafts to pump.

Their saliva added to the sounds of wetness between the four men, and with only a single eye peeked open, the scene was making me firm under my bathing suit. I had seen this play out before. In the place we used to call home when I'd walk through the front door to a version of the same group play but make a straight line to my room in order to avoid it. It wasn't that it wasn't hot then, but when sex still felt like a chore, I had always declined any verbal, or nonverbal, invitation to join.

Maybe it was the wine, but something felt different this time as I watched Brent stand over Sonny and bend low enough to fit his cock into his mouth. Sonny enthusiastically turned his head and opened wide, ready to have his face used while Darius continued bobbing between his thighs.

The other brother stood and soon Marco was behind Darius, using the precum from his dripping foreskin to spread on Darius's ass and wiggle a finger in the opening. Marco straddled his thick legs and dripped spit to the round cheeks and hairy hole between his knees. When he slowly worked his cock inside, Darius moaned and hummed on Sonny's cock which caused a ripple of excited sounds through the connected line of men.

I wasn't sure if anyone could see, but I was rock hard. Some part of me felt stupid for never taking advantage of living with such attractive men who seemed to desire me. It had taken until now, when it was forbidden, for me to return that desire. Now, I wanted them more than ever.

I wanted to be behind Marco or hovering above Sonny, letting him lick between the two dicks while I kissed Brent and stroked the thick fur on his stomach. In my head, I imagined myself next to Darius on the chair, our bodies pressed together and making the plastic strips stretch down to the deck below under our combined weight. I could almost taste Sonny on me while I thought about what it would be like to kiss his precum from Darius's lips.

Where I still lay on the nearby lounge chair, I could see the long-haired man, flat on his back, reaching his hand between the standing man's legs. Sonny tickled at Brent's balls then sucked on his own fingers to bring the spit between Brent's ass cheeks and shove it into his hole.

As he was penetrated, Brent spotted me watching the scene unfold and smirked. He nodded and smiled, looking down to his brother on the other end of the orgy pile. I'd never fucked either of the brothers. But, admittedly, despite my generally mixed feelings about their stupidity in general life and conversation, they were both incredibly sexy.

The wine swirled in my stomach, mimicking butterflies. I felt nervous and excited—as if in this place I was seeing the men in a whole new way. Basking in the stained glass of the atrium, the stone men, the art, and blue water reflecting in all of their eyes, I wanted them all. But as I prepared to stand and join the group, in an instant, my stomach went sour. I froze where I lay, paralyzed by the vow I'd made. The promise we'd all cemented the moment we accepted Usher into our bodies. We didn't belong to ourselves anymore.

We belonged to Usher. We served the house.

Despite my better judgement and realization, my hand still found its way to my cock and I stroked, watching the men suck and fuck each other. A quick switch of positions and Darius was on his stomach with Sonny behind him, working several fingers inside the now widened hole, loosened by Marco's girthy uncut dick. The brothers hovered to the sides, pumping tip to base until Sonny moved to the side to let Brent into his place fucking Darius. Sonny was immediately on his knees and swallowing Marco to the hilt over and over again while he gripped and pulled at his own dick.

Now facing me while Brent pounded him from behind, Darius was next to spot me watching. He followed the motion of my strokes under the thin material of my bathing suit. Rubbing my precum over the more sensitive skin of my head, I was close to releasing. Everything was building and pulsing, ready to explode. The sounds echoing through the massive atrium built into a crescendo of moans; we were all ready. Darius reached his hand toward me and smiled, pulling at the waistband of the short trunks again. I didn't stop him.

With my cock exposed to the humid air from the enclosed pool and sex, my balls tightened seeing Darius's fist prepare to grip me. With only a few pumps, I knew I would shoot. But in that exact moment, as the eruption of our collective climax began, the house shook and vibrated with something sinister. My body clenched, and we all stopped.

Standing in the strange vibrating earthquake of knowing we were about to be caught, the feeling was undeniable. Usher had returned.

CHAPTER SIX

❧

T he slamming of a single door sent a shockwave through the manor. I felt sheer panic, unsure whether to clean the mess, hide, or just stand frozen and accept the consequences.

Knowing he was back hit like a swift punch to my stomach as I looked around at the merlot and cabernet stains around the pool, the dirty underwear and towels balled up in the corners. I thought about the wet footprints we'd left through just about every accessible room over the course of a week and could already sense Usher in the grand foyer calculating our punishment for desecrating his home.

I had not made sure they boys behaved themselves. Now, they were experiencing the same fear I'd held inside of me for too long. The men scrambled to their feet and grabbed up what they could hold in their arms while wiping precum and spit from their cocks and holes.

Darius huffed, dabbing a spilled pinot noir from the porous cement. "Girl, help us!" he yelled as he continued to pat the full-sized towel frantically over the moisture.

I didn't move other than slipping my softening cock back into my shorts. Putting my arms behind my head as a pillow on the lounger, I breathed in deeply and exhaled. The damage had already been done.

We'd been entering the atrium each day through the new bookcase but directly across from it were the double set of doors Roderick had showed me. Those same doors shook and burst open, revealing Usher with two shorter figures on either side of him. One was Roderick, wearing real clothes for the first time since we'd reconnected. His outfit looked fierce, but his face was predictably judgmental above his tight sheer shirt and black pants. He folded his arms, cocked his head to the side, and smirked at me as if he knew something I didn't.

On the other side was a young man so handsome all of the boys stopped their frantic cleaning. Sonny gasped and the bundle of bottles he'd collected fell to the ground. On impact, they shattered into hundreds of emerald and crystal shards around everyone's bare feet. As they stood naked, surrounded by the broken glass, all of the boys' eyes were on Usher. No one moved. I exhaled again.

Already I could feel the familiar sting of whips and hear the silence of impending solitude. Soon enough, I'd meet the rubber gloves and be on my knees scrubbing marble statues, probably using small abrasive brushes to clean the spots behind their finely-chiseled ball sacks.

In a way, those were the options I preferred after seeing the harsh cage Roderick had been equipped with after disobeying Usher. I couldn't tell if he still had it on, but just thinking about not having access to my own cock made me squirm where I lay.

That sort restriction from even my own hand used to cross a line in my brain. But now, the way my kinks had a way of pushing the threshold of what seemed sexy further and further from what once turned me on, I knew if Usher put the chastity device on me, I would wear it. If he poked and prodded my nuts and made me wait to cum until he rewarded me with the key, I would say thank you and ask for more. As long as it pleased him.

Even from several yards away I could see, the newest boy at Usher's side had eyes that sparkled under perfectly arched eyebrows. His lashes curved in just the right way too. Framing his thick lips, he had a jawline sharper than the pieces of jagged glass protruding from the crimson puddle creeping down the pool deck in Usher's direction. It had become a red blend of alcohol and mistakes no one felt like drinking anymore.

The suited man watched the liquid drip like blood in a single running line until it stopped in front of him. As conflicted and angry as I was knowing he'd taken Roderick on his trip instead of me, I still thought Usher looked incredibly hot between the two shorter men. Rugged but shaped facial hair surrounded his lips. He bit the thickness of the bottom portion then pressed them together, surveying everything. The mess. The nakedness. The very obvious sex that had taken place.

Even if he hadn't witnessed it remotely, the scent of cum hung in the air along with smashed fermented grapes, sweat, and chlorine. A silence stretched eerily with everyone frozen in place. Our fates were sealed. We were ready for the verdict to be delivered by the master of the house, standing steady, inhaling our missteps.

Then he smiled. "Well. Did you boys have a good time?" Usher lifted his head in our direction and ran a finger across one brow.

My stomach dropped. His attempt at humor couldn't be sincere. This was worse than I'd anticipated. I wanted everyone in the room gone so I could beg him for forgiveness with his beautiful cock in my mouth. So I could feel him touch me and hold me. So we could really talk.

Above the handsome grin, his mustache curled toward his cheeks. He flashed straight white teeth. Something unsaid lingered in the space between the two groups of men. An impending battle. Whatever happened next was going to be terrible.

No one moved from their position, but the deep breaths I'd been taking had spread to the naked side of the room. The other four boys inhaled in odd synchronicity nearby while the pyramid of men in the doorway stood firm. With a quick exhale, Darius unexpectedly spoke, "I'm sorry. We—"

He was cut off immediately by Usher's booming voice bouncing from the textured walls and statuesque men filling the decorated space, "Enough. Let's not be rude to our guest, boy."

Usher motioned a graceful hand toward the new handsome young man. The one wearing tailored jeans that hugged his fit body. From the V-neck of his shirt, a tuft of thick chest hair curled its way over the fabric. Even from where I sat, his nipples were erect enough to push through the cotton.

I could tell by the way he held himself—one leg crossed over the other, the toe of his shoe resting on the ground, a hand in his pocket while the other pushed swooping hair back in place—he knew every man in that room wanted to fuck him. Even more so, this wasn't a new feeling; he radiated a breed of confidence that took years of compliments to cultivate.

By the way Usher looked at the new addition as he posed so aloofly, it seemed no man among us wanted to fuck the fresh meat more than Usher. No matter how attractive and self-assured the new boy was, I immediately wanted to hate him.

"Upstairs, all of you. We don't have the time for this." Usher pushed the sleeve of his pressed suit back and looked at his gold watch. He wasn't smiling anymore. "We're already behind schedule."

Usher looked at me where I still lay stupefied on the lounge chair. When he pursed his lips and shook his head to demonstrate his disappointment, I was glad not to have my dick out.

Being naked while he clicked his tongue and wagged his finger at me could have gone in either direction.

Almost anytime his eyes were on me, I seemed to get a little hard, but disappointing him made something retreat under the safety of my shorts. Then, before turning on his heels to exit the atrium, he waited for the other boys to look away. With one side of his mouth curved up, as though he were amused, he winked.

It seemed the gesture had only been for me. If it hadn't, no one else had noticed the quick eye movement. Something had happened wherever he had been for the last week. From even the brief interaction, I could tell he seemed excited to be home. He was happy to see us, or at the very least, me.

Whether that meant we would bypass harsh punishment for our actions, I didn't know. But what I did know was I didn't entirely recognize the man who had returned. His face and body were the same, but his softened expressions and warmth felt fraudulent.

It could have been a performance intended to disarm us, or perhaps he really was actually in a good mood. Either way, the uncertainty had me on edge. Walking from the chair and leaving the desecrated indoor pool behind, the world I'd known here suspended above the unknown, and I found myself bracing for impact.

CHAPTER SEVEN

❧

How there was a hand-written note waiting on my bed the second I opened the door, I had no idea. As far as I knew, Usher and his jet-setting sidekicks had arrived only moments before they'd burst into the atrium. But, like most things in the mansion, there was often something I was missing.

Not only was there a note. With no one watching, I'd stopped picking up after myself days ago. Yet my bed was made, my bathtub was scrubbed, and all the clothes in my closet were clean and pressed. So much housekeeping had been accomplished. Maybe I had been drunk and asleep longer than I thought.

Whipping off the wet wine and precum doused trunks, I stood nude in my newly cleaned room as I unfolded the note.

Clean yourself.
Orange jockstrap.
Dining room.

In another life before joining the house, I'd gone to a party that handed out colored bandanas at the door. The large security guard would size you up before entering. He'd look at your clothes and hands; analyze your shoes and mouth. Then he'd hand you a color from a plastic trash bag packed tight with a cascade of rainbow polyester.

Back then, he slid something vibrant orange through his closed fist like a magician doing a party trick. The massive authority figure turned me around by the waist in a swift motion. Pulling at my ass to make space in my back-left pocket, he stuck the bandana in, letting half of it visibly dangle.

When I asked him what it meant and what others would know about me simply from the color protruding from my cut-off jeans, he said, "Anything. Anytime."

Like a queer fortune teller with runes or illustrated cards telling a customer about a prosperous future, I wanted to believe his intuition was correct.

Even though I was yet to discover new bubbles since adding them to Darius's go-bag that was most likely lost somewhere in the woods, the purple bathtub felt welcoming. I could have stayed submerged with my toes curling over the edge all night, but as the classical music shifted to something dark and moody, I knew it was calling for me to pick up the pace.

I was still aching to cum from my partial participation in the pseudo-orgy. While I dried every part of my body outside of the wardrobe, I thought about finishing myself off. In case I arrived in the dining room to the bad news that Usher knew we had all touched each other while he was away—then presented the worse news in the form of a strict enclosure around my cock locked with a single key—I wanted to get off one last time on my own terms.

As if it were a dream I had abruptly been awoken from, I imagined what would have happened had Usher not stopped us. At the thought of Darius stroking me while the other boys fucked him, sucking the brothers and Sonny, us all cumming hard together, my cock was standing firm while I dried my hair.

I reached down to stroke, but the moment I had the shaft in my fist, the music seemed louder than before. Then even louder. Then louder still. I dropped my grip. Not only because it was impossible to concentrate with blaring violin concertos and classical piano recitals in my ear, but because I knew how to take a hint. Someone didn't want me to cum, and rather than tempt fate for more punishment, I opened the drawers in the wardrobe and found the orange jockstrap.

On my way down the stairs, I didn't see the other boys come out of their rooms. The lights were dim and night had fallen outside. Under my feet, the cold tile felt familiar and reminded me of the first time I had officially met with Usher. How he had approached me from behind and grabbed me by the hair. The way he had inserted himself into me in spite of his intentions to keep a separation between us.

No matter how many boys filled the rooms now, that was still something only he and I shared. The warmth of his occasional intimacy kept me tiptoeing to my destination even though I was afraid of what I was about to encounter. Whether I ended up gagged or bruised, tied or confined, he had called me by my name before he left. Even if I was "boy" when we weren't alone, I still knew, in his eyes, I was special. That fact was all I had to hold onto when I reached the bottom step and let the flickering taper candles guide my way to the dining room.

Taking the lit path, I passed the area where Roderick and I had crawled on all fours to the red room together. Where we'd been connected by a single leash at our collars and I had felt like he was the only thing I wanted in the universe. Then, I'd needed to ease his pain. I'd needed to feel his body and lips. Usher had seemed like the enemy that night, but the only adversary I had in the manor now was Roderick.

The candles continued into the archway, but as I entered, things in the dining area looked different. The mess of used plates, forks, and silver trays had disappeared. Chairs and tables had been replaced with thick rugs and pillows.

Seeing the alterations made me realize any bit of destruction we'd left throughout the house had been remedied. Everything was spotless and pristine again. I wondered if I'd lost track of time in the bathtub, but before I could attempt to calculate how even a group of housekeepers could have gotten everything back in order during a quick wash and wardrobe change, a voice was behind me.

"Deliciously spooky," Marco said, posing near the fiery glow in a dark blue jockstrap. Next to him, his brother leaned on his shoulder in contrasting bright pink.

From the kitchen, Darius emerged with Sonny behind him. Sonny tapped at Darius's framed ass in the green backless underwear and laughed.

"You're gonna get us in more trouble," Darius said, swatting at Sonny's waist near a fluorescent yellow band. Before he could respond, a creaking sound came from the corner, and a door I'd never seen before opened into the dining room.

Coming through what looked like yet another secret passage was the new boy dressed in his own black jock. All of our eyes were on him as he slowly closed the passage. He was silent as he approached before he exhaled and swung his arms at his sides. "This place, huh?" he said with an accent I couldn't place right away.

When he reached out his hand to introduce himself to the cluster of mostly naked men, I could see his fingernails were painted to match his underwear. He had just the slightest charcoal smear under his eyes to accent smokey grey irises with flecks of turquoise.

"Julien," he said and formally shook each hand before pushing his shaggy black hair behind his ears. He was rock star hot. And as much as I wanted to dislike him because he had somehow captured Usher's attention enough to have brought him all the way from what sounded like... France? Julien was, admittedly, really easy to look at.

The other boys smirked and looked at each other. Brent and Marco were especially infatuated and probably would have been banging him from either side with their lizard brains had it not been for the next sound entering the candlelit space.

From behind them, in time with the music, Usher and Roderick appeared. It seemed everyone had arrived in pairs aside from myself and Julien. In this duo, Roderick had on a deep purple jockstrap, matching his collar, and held an oval chafing dish complete with chrome lid.

He walked in front of Usher like a horse pulling a carriage. Two metal loops hooked to Roderick's neck, and on the other end, Usher held a set of reigns in one hand. He gave the lines a quick snap with a flick of his wrist.

Roderick jerked at the motion, and halted in place in front of us. He held the large tray with his forearms stretched out, presenting it.

"Well, this seems about right doesn't it, boys?" Usher detached the strips from Roderick's collar and threw them to the side of the room beyond the pillows. "The ambiance is there, but something is missing."

Usher closed his eyes and tapped his temple as if he were recalling a memory. The music shifted from haunting piano to a single violin that ebbed and flowed with notes of longing. Usher kept his eyes closed, but smiled. "Yes, there you are."

I didn't see him reach into his pocket or anywhere else to use the remote I'd seen him use before to control the atmosphere of any room, but nothing about him and his need to be mysterious surprised me anymore. It had been timed somehow, the shift, and while I was impressed by his dedication to keep the experience interesting, so much of me wanted to live behind the curtain.

When he opened his eyes again, they seemed glossy, and he inhaled deeply, stifling some sort of emotion. The moment was fleeting as all of us stood together with our hairy asses exposed to the open air. I wanted to sit on one of the large cushions covering the floor, which I was certain Roderick appreciated. They reminded me of his tweed floor poufs and the way he tried to pass them off as actual furniture.

But before I could entertain the idea of continuing to nurse my hangover from our week-long bender, Usher was lifting the lid of the shiny dish. Roderick's arms shook under the weight, and I wondered why he was always being punished with such tedious physical training. He did seem to be developing a certain endurance. If he was in pain, it didn't show on his face.

If anything, he appeared pleased when Usher presented the contents of his offering to all of us: colorful ropes wrapped into coils. All were different: purple, pink, green, yellow, black, blue, and orange.

Chapter Eight

It didn't make sense to me at first, but next to the wrapped cords was a single paddle, flat and wide. No one moved. Usher nodded to the vibrant colors on the tray then to our hips and between our legs. He was bringing our attention to the waistbands and pouches, the strips of elastic cupping our furry ass cheeks.

"Take your color, boys," Usher said with a sinister smile, sliding the wooden paddle from the tray before sauntering to the other side of the room. He tapped it against his palm and leaned against the wall, closing his eyes to take in the music.

The boys hovered in a semi-circle around the options. With Usher almost out of earshot, Roderick whispered through strained breath, "Hurry up." His arms trembled, and he shifted his weight back and forth on his feet.

Surprisingly, it was Sonny who made the connection first. Glancing down at his blindingly yellow underwear and matching it with the corresponding rope on the platter, he palmed the coils and strutted between the pillows like an obstacle course. We hadn't been instructed to, but after Sonny sat down on a cushion and began unraveling the rope ball, the remainder of us followed his lead.

Usher didn't speak while Roderick retired the empty tray and settled with his matching purple rope on the floor with us. He massaged his tired arms. With our lines unwrapped, Usher opened his eyes only to say to no one in particular, "Doesn't he play beautifully?"

Nervously twisting the orange rope around my fingers, I wasn't familiar with the artist of the piece flowing from the speakers in the house. But Usher was right; the music was beautiful.

For whatever was about to happen, the mood had been set, and he allowed us to bask in it for a few more minutes as the violin continued to play its ominous score. When a piece ended and drifted into a moment of silence, Usher audibly sighed and sauntered to the center of where we were perched on the grouping of pillows.

"Up," he said quickly and gestured for us to rise. When we stood, he nodded to Roderick who hastily grabbed Marco's rope from him then turned him by the shoulders. "Hands behind your back, boy," Usher said, observing Marco's apprehension at being handled so roughly by another boy.

Still, Marco obeyed Usher's order and allowed Roderick to loop the dark blue line around his wrists. He winced as Roderick tied the rope off tightly and looked at the group of us watching.

"All of you," Usher said, nodding to the lines in our hands. A collective hesitation fell across us, but it only lasted a few seconds before we fumbled around, trading the colored ties.

It felt strange trying to decide which man to present my rope to, but Julien approached me before I had the chance to choose. I still wanted to hate him. Even in that moment, I could see Usher staring at Julien's plump furry ass as he bent over to fasten my wrists. His touch was gentle. As the fur on his arms brushed against my lower back, I thought about how badly I wanted to cum.

Only Roderick was left to be secured, and Usher took the purple rope firmly in his hand before pushing his collared boy against the closest surface. Roderick's face pressed to the egg-shell wall with Usher's elbow across his back to hold him in place as he was tied. The swift motion was so aggressive the rest of us jumped back. I nearly tripped on a floor pillow, and it made me wonder what I would have done if I had landed on the hardwood panels without a way to get back on my feet without humiliating myself. Perhaps that was the intention. He wanted us to be helpless.

The sudden force Usher was demonstrating extended past the interaction with Roderick. Moving from the wall, he returned to the middle of the dining area and kicked each floor cushion out of the way. "Circle up," he said with hostility in his voice. "Face the outside."

I was nervous again. His constantly shifting mood surged adrenaline through my body, tensing me in a rapid cycle. Usher breathed in deeply as if he were trying to prepare for something, then I felt it.

On my ass framed in the orange jockstrap, something thundered against my skin. It immediately burned so intensely I was certain all of the air had left my body forever.

A storm of rapid hits followed the echo of the first contact, but not on me. Usher was making his way around the circle of boys, putting paddle to bare ass over and over again. I could see from my peripheral vision that when a boy seemed to be losing his balance from the pain, he'd stand them up straight again and continue.

The music ascended with furious stings. As the anguish grew, an image came into my head of a boy playing the violin in time with our percussion. He strummed the chords out in succession, and as the track ended, my premonition blended into the agony of my reality. As my skin scorched, flames surrounded the young musician. He looked into my eyes and whispered, "Run."

I was in the room again. Candles wavered in reflections on the wet faces of every boy I could see by turning my head in either direction. Usher had gone around the circle with his paddle at least a dozen times based on the multitude of spots where my ass burned red hot.

He must have tired himself out because he stood hunched over in his suit before dropping the paddle to the polished wood floor. During his break, he walked to a small table nearby that I hadn't noticed before. From a decanter, he poured and sipped a glass of red wine.

While he caught his breath, the seven of us stayed in formation, afraid to move. I kept my legs parted in a wide stance to keep my raw cheeks from touching each other as much as possible. Either a drop of sweat or a tear rolled from my face to my chest where it settled in my fur.

Seemingly refreshed and back in the center of our circle, Usher spoke firmly, "Now the front, boys."

Hesitation no longer seemed to be an option after the pain had broken down my defenses. I spun my throbbing backside away from the man in control and offered him my cock which was still safely resting in the orange jockstrap.

With a clear view of each other and our hands still tied behind our backs, Usher traveled to every boy and wiggled the band of our underwear down to our ankles. I'd seen the cocks in that room before, aside from Julien, who hung long even when he was soft.

It wasn't long before I got to see that the young French man could grow even larger when he was hard as Usher spit in his own hand and began stroking him from base to tip. "Don't cum," Usher said to the boy, loud enough for us all to hear.

After a few minutes, Julien wiggled in place trying to escape the milking. He clenched his teeth and winced. Usher stopped. The French man's cock still stood at attention when Usher moved onto Brent. Julien sighed with relief.

Using the same tactic, the older man cycled through each boy the way he had with the paddle, but instead of inflicting pain, he was edging us over and over again.

From the second he gripped me with his lubricated fist when my turn came around, I wished I had ignored the music and jerked-off before coming down the stairs. I'd spilled my load before Usher had wanted me to in the past and suffered the consequences. I wasn't going to make the same mistake.

By his third time around the circle, I was biting my lip hard and squirming from his touch. Letting up, Usher swatted at my cock and smirked. Quiet enough so no one else could hear, he said, "Just a little longer, boy."

It was Brent who came first, his droplets landing to the floor below. Then Sonny, who didn't seem to care very much about losing whatever competition was going on as long as he could relax again soon. Darius gave in, then Marco. Sticky pearls gathered like an abstract painting in front of each boy across the dark wooden floor.

I couldn't take my eyes off of Julien's cock while Usher stroked it furiously. He ran his hand up Julien's furry abs and chest until he reached his mouth, "Spit, boy." When Julien complied, Usher brought the warm liquid down to continue pumping. The French man was close.

"Beautiful," Usher said, when Julien arched his head back and finally exploded. Even losing whatever strange game we were playing, Usher somehow still found him perfect.

With only Roderick and myself left, our keeper motioned for us to meet in the middle of the circle. He untied both our colored cords and placed our hands on each other's cocks. My wrists throbbed from being released, and my balls pulsed with a mix of pleasure and anger. We knew each other's weaknesses, and as badly as I wanted to cum, I was even more determined to beat him.

Roderick ran his finger from just above my balls and all the way to my tip while I rubbed the flatness of my palm on the underside of him, where I knew he was most sensitive. We stared into each other's eyes with something that made me want to breathe fire. It was passion mixed with betrayal, anger mixed raw sexuality. I wanted to take him down.

There was something in him that felt just as relentless. He wouldn't release my gaze. And for a moment his eyes softened, almost like an apology.

As I had my guard down to process the meaning behind his look, he stroked faster. The crowd of boys and their spent cocks watched intensely, former a tighter circle around our battle. Usher was stoic at our side like a referee, paddle in hand, prepared to step in at any time.

I tensed up but worried it was too late. I tried to think about unsexy things, but all I could see was the visible anticipation of six attractive men focused on my hard cock. I heard the paddle slapping against Usher's hand and thought about the last time I'd held him in my mouth.

At the point of no return, I came hard on Roderick's hand. He smiled before taking a few steps back and shaking my load from his fingers to the ground.

CHAPTER NINE

W e'd been dismissed to our separate rooms after the new group ritual. Although I didn't understand it entirely, Usher seemed amused by the outcome. He also stood around for a few minutes once I'd came, looking at the ceiling and through the windows but not sharing with us what he was searching for. The suited man appeared nervous, bracing himself for something which never arrived.

All in all, I was happy to be alone again. Having friends around had been nice, but when a tray arrived for breakfast the next morning, I was relieved I wouldn't have to go back downstairs. I wasn't in any hurry to see Usher either while my stinging ass healed from being swatted over and over again with the paddle.

Days passed outside my small window when, one night, something called to me. A voice I'd never heard in the house before woke me from a deep sleep. It drew me down the stairs like a siren before I knew even I was walking. Now, I was standing in front of the stone figure guarding the entrance to the control room. The secret words fell from my mouth into his stone ear, and he slid to the side, granting me passage to the already unlocked room.

CHAPTER NINE

Curtains had been drawn from inside the dungeon to block out the two way mirror. I pushed the button to open the mic on the other side and heard what sounded like a conversation at first. Two voices went back and forth, but they weren't discussing anything as much as trading the incoherent grunts and dirty talk people do when they're having sex. But hearing Usher's cadence and tone among the two, I knew that couldn't be what was happening in the red room.

Through the velvet drapes of the portrait room, I didn't take the time to greet the painted men before bending down to feel around for the opening to the panel Usher had revealed to me behind the pegboard holding toys only days before.

When my fingers found the crack, I pushed lightly and peeked one eye through the opening. In the new sling, Sonny was on his back, legs in the air, furry toes against the chain. Usher stood in front of him, and from where I spied, I had a full view of them both.

I watched as Usher took out his hard cock but still didn't believe what I was seeing. He tapped his hardness on the suspended boy and using his tip, rubbed the precum from Sonny's front hole all over both their dicks. The surfer moaned with pleasure of the frottage before Usher moved his moist cock head to Sonny's ass to tease the opening. Sonny stroked his dick between two fingers while the man standing above him pushed just slightly into one hole, then the other, never fully entering.

The sleepy boy with the wavy beach hair had always been a favorite of the men who came to the old house. Not in a fetishy way—Sonny was just exceptional in bed. He'd told us before that having three fuckable holes didn't automatically make him a bottom. As much as he liked to get fucked, he'd always favored being versatile. Having an option the rest of us didn't have, and making his own lube, made him unique.

Sometimes when he was stoned enough, he'd laugh and tell us, "Sorry about your luck." Then he'd throw back his luscious mane and parade his perfect ass around the boardwalk. No one needed to know what was in his pants unless they were planning to fuck him, but once most men saw him tossing his board around the waves, that's exactly what they wanted.

Usher had apparently found him just as irresistible because right in front of me, he wasn't just inserting toys or hitting flesh. Sony wasn't receiving him at the end of a paddle or riding crop. The man who said fucking wasn't the way things were done in the house, the one who chastised me for making him break his own rules, was on the cusp of penetrating Sonny's holes.

It was only teasing for a while, but when Usher finally pushed inside, they both moaned and Sonny pulled at the chain. The standing man's eyes rolled back as he thrust in and out of one hole and moved to the other, back and forth, coating his fur in slippery precum. The sling rocked back and forth, making it easier for his entire length to be swallowed by the hairy openings.

My heart sank. I closed the panel and leaned back against the wall below a hanging portrait. The men in the room, their faces illuminated by a spotlight, seemed to be mocking me. With my head between my bent knees, my face felt warm and my body went empty with embarrassment. How could I have been so stupid to think I was the only one Usher was having sex with?

Slowly, I pushed the panel again and focused my sight through the slots in the pegboard. I didn't want to force it too far this time and have one of the thin metal rods or double-ended dildos fall to the cement, giving me away. Through the dots I could see a swiss cheese version of their encounter, but the score was still clear. The moans of pleasure and rattling of chains. Slaps to Sonny's chest and the back of his thighs as Usher went feral, forcing himself deeper and deeper.

At least they weren't kissing. Not that we had either, but seeing Usher's lips touch another man may have broken me in that moment.

Still observing the scene, I watched Usher grab Sonny's cock and stroke it while they fucked. He wanted him to have a good time, to enjoy it. He jerked it hard until they came together. And in that exact moment, my stomach felt sick.

Usher was slumped over Sonny's body on the sling, and I closed the panel to return to the ball I'd been sitting in. I worried that if I kept watching, I'd see him stay. The way he finally had with me after leaving his load inside my body so many times. Sonny already had Usher's warmth, and now I worried he had his attention.

I crawled my way back through the red curtains on my hands and knees. The mic was still open in the control room, broadcasting a rhythmic panting. I couldn't tell if it was one man or two catching their breath post energetic coitus, but I didn't want to find out. With a quick flip, the sound was gone, and I sat alone in the silence.

From the roll top desk across from me, a drawer protruded from the middle section. I didn't remember it being pulled out on my way in, but I had, admittedly, been mostly asleep. When I crawled over, I saw that the folder Roderick had shown me weeks before with our names and images was inside, opened to a page with a face and set of stats I hadn't seen in there the first time.

Just below Julien's picture, not far from text detailing the location he'd been found in France, his known sexual skills, and a generally high rating of obedience was a familiar word:

Novitiate

I still wasn't sure want the seemingly ancient title meant in relation to our adorable little sex cult fraternity of furry men, but when I flipped the complied book back a page, Roderick's glossy bearded face was staring back. Under his name was the word:

Postulant

Slamming the folder back into the drawer, there were assumptions I could make. One was that among all of the boys, Roderick and Julien were at the top of the list. If I'd ventured further into the pages, I was certain I would have seen Sonny somewhere as well.

The other assumption was that the ranking Usher was keeping could change at any time, and right now, my position was slipping. If I was on it at all anymore, I was apparently not at the top of his list for favorite boys.

CHAPTER TEN

I t took me until mid-afternoon, when food didn't arrive at my door, to drag my growling stomach down to the kitchen in search of sustenance. I could hear talking before I even turned the corner into the sitting room with the bookcase leading the kitchen. The chatter made me wish I was alone again, that they would all disappear, and I could return to my solitude—just so I wouldn't have to explain myself.

Julien was wedged between Brent and Marco on one of the sofas with the tufted back. It was definitely an antique and older than all of us; it would be impossible to have it cleaned.

Brent ran his finger down Julien's bare chest and down his stomach. "So France?" he asked. Julien nodded. "You must know a lot about Eiffel Towers then."

The brothers laughed at the joke Julien definitely didn't understand.

"Maybe you call it something else? Like whatever you call French fries there," Marco suggested with a tilted hand and a shrug before leaning in closer to the man in the middle.

Brent raised the volume of his voice as if that would make it easier for Julien to parse out and followed up by asking, "Since you travel a lot, maybe you're more familiar with the London Bridge?"

The French boy cleared his throat nervously, looking back and forth at the two men ready to pound him from both sides as soon as they got the word.

From the passage, the bookcase slid to the side and Darius emerged. "Maybe he calls it what the rest of us do: a spit roast. Speaking of which, looks like I'm banned from the kitchen. Someone else is cooking today."

He was talking to the group of men, the three about to gang-bang on priceless furniture and Sonny, whom I hadn't noticed when I walked in, passed out with his arm over his face on the matching loveseat.

When Darius saw me standing in the doorway, he put his hands on his hips, "Oh, she has risen."

I couldn't understand why we all had free reign of the house. After spending weeks locked away by myself before the arrival of the other boys, it didn't seem fair. Rage built inside of me, and seeing Sonny casually curled up after what I had witnessed the previous evening was making me burn even hotter.

"I don't travel," Julien said. The response seemed delayed as if he'd been searching for the correct English words. "His plane was the first."

"*His* plane?" Darius said, closing the bookcase behind him. "Didn't know we had our own airline too. Alexander found us some *money* money." He smiled at me, trying to make me smile back. I didn't.

"He found me at the house," Julien continued. There was something oddly serious in his tone, and for just a moment, the brothers pulled back. "People used to say the ruins were haunted. It was burned a long time ago."

"In France?" It wasn't my intention to speak to any of them, but I needed to verify where Usher went and what exactly drew him there. Would he really travel across the ocean just for a new plaything?

Julien nodded and wiped at the remnants of his smokey eyeliner. He picked at his chipping black nails then motioned to the house around us. "Like this one, but destroyed."

The French boy had been brought here from his home on an entirely different continent and was doing his best to communicate with us. He'd obviously been through a lot. I wondered if maybe I'd been too hard on him.

Darius walked farther into the room to perch on the arm of the loveseat where Sonny slept. He stroked Sonny's mane while he watched Brent and Marco poke at Julien again. They rubbed at his hairy thighs, and Julien squirmed in his seat.

"Stop bugging that kid," Darius said and snapped his fingers. He pointed toward either side of the couch, telling them to separate like unruly children. "He's obviously smarter than the two of you combined. Even if he wants to be the filling to the little croissanwich you're trying to make, he's not trying to break the rules."

"Oh, we've got rules now?" I smirked at Darius, who only days before was trying to jerk me off by the pool during a five man orgy while I resisted.

How things had changed.

"It helps to know what he wants, now that he's actually told me," Marco said, bringing his large feet up to the glass coffee table and crossing his legs at the ankle. There was something about the way he used the word "me" that made my stomach feel uneasy.

"He likes to tell us separately, I guess," Brent brought his own wide soles up and set them on Julien's lap. The French boy sighed with defeat and started stroking Brent's leg lightly with his fingertips.

"Whatever. I was getting bored fucking y'all anyway," Darius said with a slight sigh. He pulled at Sonny's ear playfully, and the cat man responded by stretching wide then balling up even tighter. "Guess no one can fuck anyone in this house except for—" Darius stopped talking when he saw my face.

"At least it's good," Marco said, filling the air. Darius nodded in agreement but didn't take his eyes off me or my obviously surprised expression.

"I thought you didn't like pain," I said. There was no way I didn't sound angry. Darius probably worried I was about to lunge myself across the room and tackle his body into the books behind him.

Darius chose his words carefully before he spoke. "Not without pleasure. No."

"Not without fucking." I wasn't asking as much as clarifying that I knew what he meant. My face burned again and the silence returned. Every boy awake in the sitting room stared at me.

In slightly broken English, Julien broke the quiet hanging between us all, "Did you think you were the only one?" he asked.

"I've been trying to tell you," a voice said from the side of the conversation. Roderick leaned in the space where the bookcase normally sat. He was the human embodiment of the judgy face emoji wearing tight underwear and giving me side eye.

When I didn't respond, he looked past me. "Food is ready," he said to everyone else. The boys stood and made their way to the kitchen, glancing at me with what could have been sympathy but was probably pity. I wanted to disappear then reappear when all of them were gone. Not just from the room, but from the house.

Darius shook Sonny's shoulder. "Food," he said in an attempt to wake him. Sonny gave a thumbs-up but didn't move from his comfortable spot.

When Darius scooted by the doorway, he reached out to put his hand on my arm, but I shrugged it away. If anyone should have told me, it was him. All of them, including Darius, needed to go.

With the room mostly cleared out, I slumped to the antique couch and put my head in my hands. All the pain I'd been taking for him, the confinement, the uncertainty—it had been for nothing. I'd not only fallen out of his favor; I didn't even deserve the truth.

I sighed heavily and wondered if I should leave the house, if I should gather the things I could call mine and try to open the wardrobe to escape into the woods. Maybe Usher was over me. Perhaps if I left, he wouldn't try to stop me. Even if I did wake up in my room again, Usher needed to know I didn't want to be here anymore. Not for the fancy things. Not for Roderick. And especially, not for him.

Sonny rolled over on the couch and cracked his eyes open. He rubbed them and waited until I realized he was awake to speak. "Sorry, dude. That sucks," he said, then turned on his side and returned to sleep.

I was going to leave. That was certain. But first, I was going to make sure Usher knew why he was losing me.

Chapter Eleven

Never even once had I thought about where Usher resided within the manor—not until I'd gone back to my room and started packing my bag. I realized then that nothing in there, aside from the clothes I'd arrived in, belonged to me.

Leaving the bag I'd started behind, I put on my old jeans, T-shirt, and boots. Stuffed in the corner of the wardrobe, they were clean but not fresh. They weren't like the clothes and gear I'd gotten used to parading in around the house, but at least they were mine.

As I prepared for my exit, a voice called my name from the hallway. I didn't know which of the other boys was outside my closed door, but I had no interest in speaking to any of them.

Opening the wardrobe, I pushed on the back panel. The lock was gone. Between where I stood and the end of the passage lay only a few hundred feet of stony path, a winding tunnel back to a life before I knew what happened inside the mansion I'd be so captivated by at one time.

I understood what Julien was telling the other men about being pulled to a place. We shared the feeling he had for the house in France which mirrored this one. Though, for some reason, that one had been burned down to the foundation.

Part of me wondered what had happened there, but more of me wanted to step my boot onto the first cobblestone below the wardrobe and never turn back.

From the hallway, the voice called my name again. It knocked in a familiar pattern. Three knocks, two knocks, one knock. *Seriously?*

Taking a breath, I stood huddled in the closet with my left sole hanging over my next decision. I could leave right now without telling anyone. Whatever Roderick was invoking our secret knock for, I wasn't interested in hearing.

He pounded out the secret signal again, this time with more force. I pulled my leg back into the wardrobe and dropped it to the carpet of my room. Speed walking from the open wardrobe and still angry, I was prepared to let Roderick receive the brunt of my displeasure.

"What?" I growled angrily, whipping open the bedroom door, prepared to see his stupid face. But there in the hallway, no one. I looked both ways up and down the corridor but not even a hint of a human man hung in the unexpected vacancy. He was messing with me.

I was ready to close my door and continue my exit plan with more rage, but something caught my eye. A painting. One of the portraits from the room with red velvet curtains had been moved and now hung at the end of the hallway.

Moving slowly toward it, I could see two men captured in the art. One was standing in a suit and the other, a younger man, knelt by his side with a collar around his neck. I knew the more youthful of the faces. Usher.

Closer now, I saw that something was different from when I had seen the painting before. The plaque below it included a name I hadn't observed the first time. The older man was footed by a gold plaque engraved with the name "Usher" while the naked and kneeling one, the man I'd come to know as Usher, was identified by a different name: Madden.

Just reading the name, my body stung with a tremendous sense of longing. The older keeper in the portrait had his sight on me, and no matter what direction I faced, his eyes followed.

Without changing positions, he seemed to be calling to me, begging for my help. "Find him," the man in the suit said. His words, in a French accent, echoed through me. My feet began shuffling on their own up the nearest staircase.

I climbed higher in the house than I had ever had access. Passages I hadn't known existed were open. Traveling over lush carpet and bracing myself with the polished banister, I ascended until the atmosphere around me grew dim.

Chandeliers hung unlit and covered with cobwebs when the stairs ran out, and I stood on what must have been the top floor. The music that typically played non-stop throughout the massive house was replaced with an eerie quiet. Twisted copper strings dangled from the upper part of the landing. Exposed and pointed wire protruded as if the speakers had been ripped from every wall.

A single door sat at the end of the platform. I approached it with caution. Every step I took made the floorboards creak under my boots and tug at my throat. I could hardly breathe or keep up with the rapid pace of my own pumping heartbeat.

Then, a few steps from the door, a flash of Usher fucking Sonny played in my brain. A series of the all the times Usher had lied to me or led me to think I was special paired with the punishment I'd taken for rules that never mattered, boiled back into fury. With that fire within me, I walked more quickly and used my anger to force open the entrance.

We gasped at the same time. Me and the naked man lying in a king-sized bed just below a porthole window. I'd seen the window from the exterior of the house. It was at the very top point of the mansion and could only be seen from the front. Before calling this castle home, I'd stared at the circular glass from outside the rusted gate. I'd grabbed the brown-red metal and wondered who could live inside such a room with only a single window. Now I had my answer.

Usher sat up quickly, his cock sitting on his thigh. He didn't attempt to cover it, and I tried not to stare. "It's your fault," Usher's voice trembled with something unfamiliar: vulnerability. The only time I'd heard anything like it before was the night he'd said my name, but never like this.

My boots tapped against the wood as I got closer to him, but for once, I didn't feel afraid. "My fault?"

"We weren't supposed to—" He stopped himself and analyzed me where I hovered near the bed. He looked at my jeans and boots. It seemed to click for him that they were my traveling clothes. My grand exit look. My escape the haunted mansion realness. "It will all be over soon."

"Because of me?" I asked, sensing a strange cynical coldness in my own voice. Weaponized and pointed.

Hanging over a chair, opposite to where I stood, Usher's suit seemed less menacing when it wasn't on him. It was not unlike the way his naked body in front of me made him seem more like a man than a constant threat. He was an attractive man, an incredibly sexy man with a hairy chest and an exceptional cock between his legs...that I was definitely looking at.

Perhaps it was the combination of the two which created such power, like a superhero with a cape and mask. Without the costume, he was someone else.

The naked man didn't answer my question. Instead, he rested his elbow on one bent knee and looked at the balled-up satin sheets surrounding him. How long had he been in this house?

"This happened before. When he loved us." Usher scrunched the soft fabric in his fist when he finally spoke. "I knew I was breaking the rules. This house will fall just like that one did."

I didn't understand the cryptic nonsense he was speaking, but it sounded ridiculous. Rolling my eyes, I felt angry again. "Yeah, okay." My arms crossed my chest on their own. "So that's why you fucked all the boys when you told me you couldn't? Because you fell in love with all of us?"

Usher sat exposed and silent for a moment, pushing again at the bedding. "No," he said but didn't look at me.

"No, you didn't fuck them?" It felt strange being direct with Usher, even if it was just my tone of voice. Impatience had taken hold, and I wanted answers. I needed to know how many men in the house had lied to me.

"Yes, I fucked them. All of them." Usher raised his head to meet my eyes, but hearing those words, I was already turning my body to leave.

One quick jolt down the steps and right out the back doors with the flowy white curtains, that's all it would take. I could bid my goodbyes to the stone men in the courtyard and be back over the tracks on the bad side of Beachside before nightfall. Maybe the old flop house was still unoccupied or Roderick's old fake apartment would be available to rent once I had the money. Until then, an alley would suffice. As long as I could get out of this house and away from everyone inside, I would be fine.

Usher leaned over quickly and grabbed my wrist, stopping my momentum. "But no. I didn't love them."

Hovering where I stood, his hand felt softer and moved from my wrist to my palm where he interwove his fingers with mine. "Why did you have to be so perfect?" he asked.

My eye caught his cock again, and as it rose from where it had been sitting against his leg, he pulled me closer to the bed. I landed next to his bare skin but tried not to touch him.

I was still upset, but my cock was getting firmer in my jeans just feeling him close. When he turned my face toward his and looked into my eyes, it was pushing at the zipper.

Pulling me in tighter by my shirt, he put his lips on mine and kissed me hard. Deep and passionate, our first kiss felt electric in a literal sense. The lights on the top floor sparked and flickered, but we didn't stop.

My cock throbbed as we rolled around the bed until I pinned him on his back to straddle his hips. Usher pulled me down to his lips, and when we finally went up for air again, he whispered, "Let it burn," then put his tongue back in my mouth.

Chapter Twelve

There were parts of him I never thought I would have the chance to explore. I licked his chest and sucked each erect nipple. He allowed me to taste and nibble his entire body and run my fingers through the fur that started just below his neck and ended at his hard cock. I tickled at his balls, and for the first time, he didn't hold back when he moaned in my ear.

"Alexander," he said, as if he knew the sound of my own name from his mouth would make me stiff. He was right.

My shirt off and my body positioned between his legs, that urge to top I hadn't felt since being with Roderick came over me like a wave rolling into an undertow. Sliding my jeans below my ass, the tip of me pushed at his hole, and I searched for the right words to open him enough to plunge inside. I ripped off my boots and pulled my jeans down to make sure he would get the full length of me.

"Madden," I said, stroking his thick cock and hoping for precum I could use as lubrication between us. The man below me jolted unexpectedly and tossed me from my stance. I fell back on the bed while he hoisted himself to his knees and towered over me.

CHAPTER TWELVE

"What did you say?" His voice had changed again. It was the tone I knew better than the despair and remorse he'd demonstrated when I'd entered the room. This was the man who had dragged me by the ankles and smacked my most sensitive parts for his enjoyment. My heart was pounding again as our naked flesh barely touched.

"Isn't that your name?" I could hear the trembling vibration of a question stuck in my throat, desperately trying to escape in time. The man I suddenly didn't know how to address leaned his ass on his heels. He brought his hands to his upper thighs and looked down at the sheets we'd unraveled in the tide of our passion. Now I was drowning in the choppy waves of his unpredictable nature.

Afraid to move from where I'd fallen, I watched him continue to kneel as if he were listening to something I couldn't hear. He ran his hands through his dark hair and rubbed his lips together, deep in thought.

I had never said his name to him before, even when I'd learned the title from seeing it around the house. He hadn't asked me to call him anything, only to comply with his demands as he made them. But in that moment, while I braced myself for an expected impact, my lips parted slowly. The word came out just above the volume of a whisper, "Usher?"

Watching his face change to anger, I immediately wished I hadn't spoken. Whatever I'd done to stop and upset him, I regretted it. We could have still been kissing. I could have been pressed against his chest and caressing the neat beard on his face. If I'd just stayed quiet, there was a chance I'd be deep inside of him, instead of fearing his next movement.

"There is no Usher. Not anymore," he finally said. I didn't understand, but that must have been clear by my facial expression as I still lay below him with my cock growing soft through the fly of my pants.

"There was one, a long time ago, but he's not me. He wasn't the man who brought me here either." The naked man moved suddenly, swinging his wide foot from the bed to the wooden floor in one quick swoop. I didn't mean to flinch and cover my balls, but it was a reflex.

He reached for his black dress socks, which lay on the floor in front of the chair near his shiny shoes. "You know more than I thought, but you still have no idea what you're part of, do you, boy?"

With his socks on, he went for his fitted black briefs next. They'd been folded into a tidy square that Usher unraveled to slip each leg through. While he brought them over his hairy ass and adjusted his balls inside, I was already missing his cock.

"I didn't know either when he brought me to France, but it's no excuse for your behavior." With each piece of clothing concealing his nudity, his tone grew harsher. I ached for the vulnerability he'd shown me for the limited few minutes when I'd first pushed through the door to the strange attic which seemed to be his room.

"How long have you been here?" I asked, unsure why I was speaking.

"You're asking the wrong question," Usher said tersely as he grabbed his linen dress pants from the back of the chair. When he fastened the button and pulled at the zipper, the lights flickered again. I assumed it was the strange wiring up here, but I was so nervous it felt as if the bed was shaking below me.

Usher steadied himself against the arm of the chair and shook his head. He reached for his belt and even in my confusion from the sudden movement around me, I blocked my chest and face with my arms, certain he would hit me with the long strip.

"I think we may be passed that now." He laughed and looped the belt through his pants, fastening it below his navel. "It's already begun, boy."

My eyes fixated on the hair resting between the silver buckle and his belly button until the rumble below me happened again. I gripped the sides of the bed. It wasn't just my nerves; the entire house was shaking.

"What's happening?" I yelled to the man slipping an arm through his white collared shirt. He buttoned the end around his wrist with a silver cufflink before he spoke calmly. "Ritual. Revenge. Retribution. I knew the moment I saw you this is how it would end."

As he followed with the other sleeve and brought the fabric to his chest to button together, the floor shook. The walls vibrated.

I jumped to my feet and glanced around for my clothes. Before I could ask if he thought it was safe to be in the old house with it moving around us, Usher was suddenly near me. Alarmingly close to my face, he brought his hand to the stubble on my cheek and stroked it lightly.

I leaned into his open palm seeking comfort and asked, "Should we leave?"

A cruel laughter erupted from the man, and without withdrawing his hand, he said, "Sure. Go ahead. Go. That was your plan, wasn't it?" He patted the side of my face, patronizing me.

Despite his sudden return to coldness, I wanted the man I'd met in this room to return. I turned my head slightly to let my lips touch his hand and kissed his fingers. My hand rose to join his and bring his hand closer to my mouth. As the house trembled and the lights flashed, I whispered quietly, "Come with me."

His hand pulled away immediately and with force, smacked against the spot on my cheek where it had been resting. The floor beneath me felt like it was about to crumble while Usher screamed loudly enough for his voice to echo across the walls, "Go now!"

Chapter Thirteen

I left my clothes and Usher in the attic. My balls slapped my thighs as I ran down the shaking stairs, pushing the cobwebs from my face. When I reached my room, I hoped to grab shorts and continue my pace straight out the back door. As I gripped the doorknob, a series of screams came from a few doors down.

The house continued to vibrate while my detour toward the sounds of terror brought me to the sitting room. There I saw three faces I recognized: Brent, Marco, and Julien. The brothers were naked and frozen in a high-five. One was in Julien's mouth and the other was behind him.

All balanced on the antique couch, the young Frenchman was on all-fours between the twins. His cock hung long and hard, but it wasn't swinging with the momentum of being fucked from both sides.

Each man in the threesome was so hard, in fact, they were stone. Statues with expressions of pleasure plastered to their scruffy faces. A trio of men fused together forever in a top-tier sexual position, turned to priceless art.

I ran. I aborted my mission to cover my naked body and sprinted from the sitting room to the staircase. At the bottom beyond the grand foyer, the double doors were open. Their white drapes were gently sucked into a light breeze framing my path to freedom. All I had to do was walk through.

I hesitated. No matter how we'd left things, I knew I needed to find the other boys and take them with me. There were so many questions, even more since my latest conversation with Usher. Among them was how I would find my friends in a crumbling house of endless mystery rooms and secret doors. In the midst of my uncertainty, something around the corner called to me and soon my feet moved again on their own.

Now the back doors were completely out of view, and I found myself in front of the control room with the stone man I'd whispered to so many times. He was looking down on me. Unlike the times he'd granted me access before, in this moment, his eyes seemed to look passed me. When I turned to see what he was focused on, a door I'd never noticed before across the hall was bathed in a strange light.

The statue shook. His muscular body quaked with the house until I reached my closed fist toward the door. Then he stopped, almost as if to tell me I was finally on the right track. I had planned to knock, but as I got closer, the room opened on its own, revealing a real man in the flesh sitting by himself.

"There you are," Roderick said, barely looking up. He seemed unaffected by the now constant jittering of the entire manor.

I hadn't realized I was close to tears before I started yelling my questions at him.

"What happened to them?"

"It was probably the twins, right? They never had a chance," he said calmly, shaking his head.

Brent and Marco weren't actually twins, but it seemed like a less than an important detail to tell Roderick as the tweed poufs in his room wavered back and forth with the rolling of the house.

The man on the floor flipped through paperwork and rummaged in binders. On his lap was the folder from the control room, the one he had shown me with our pictures and descriptions. He opened it to cross reference something from another book.

"Julien too? Huh." He shrugged and with a red marker drew two crossed lines over Julien's face on the page. From where I stood dick-out and almost crying in his doorway, I couldn't see if Roderick was smiling.

"Unexpected," he continued and tapped the marker at the section of file with Julien's perfect ass captured on film and fastened with a paperclip above his stats. "The only candidate from the other house already taken down." Roderick turned the page.

"We need to find Darius and Sonny and get out of here!" I yelled as a piece of Roderick's ceiling fell to the floor next to him, leaving plaster dust on his hairy leg. He brushed it off and continued rifling through the papers and pictures.

"It's all right here," Roderick said, poking his marker at a page with both of our photos on it. "Everything is happening the way it was supposed to happen."

"You sound just like him. Have either of you heard of a self-fulfilling prophecy?" If the house hadn't been falling down around us, I would have crossed my arms.

Roderick smirked. "You always were the smart one, weren't you?" He was finally looking at my face, but then his eyes were on my cock. If he hadn't realized I was naked before, he knew now. "Come over here."

Terror was doing something strange to my body. In Roderick's room, the one I'd searched for only weeks before, I wasn't that far from the back door. I could just start running again. There was a chance the other boys had already found their way out. But for some reason, I was getting incredibly hard, and being anxious only made me thicker.

When I moved from the doorframe and through the maze of cushions toward him, it wasn't because I felt any safer. The house continued to shake and bits of dust sprinkled from above.

Roderick got to his feet, leaving the paperwork and books scattered around us. He pulled his shirt over his head and let his shorts fall to his ankles. Just as turned on as I was, he pressed his chest into mine and let our hard cocks push against each other.

"It was always going to be us. We were always the golds." His words made me think about the first day we met. When we sat on a picnic table at the beach painting shells in bright colors. The ones that had to be the best to receive a shimmering coat.

"This may be our last chance," he whispered. Through Roderick's lashes, his eyes sparkled with something I'd so often mistaken for sincerity. All the information on the ground, the way he always seemed to know what was coming next—even before I'd arrived, he'd been calculating.

Even knowing that, when he ran his hand over the curve of my ass and said, "I tried my best to keep you safe," I chose to believe he meant it.

A firm grip around my cock and stroking, I reached toward him and mirrored his motion. His lips on mine still tasted like the ocean, the one I never thought I would miss when I left it behind.

Both of our precum tasted just as salty as that beach when I reached up to my mouth for spit to slide between us. With our cocks stacked on top of each other, we jerked them together and thrust into our closed palms. Our parts frotted and writhed while we kissed each other's necks and chests.

"Forgive me," Roderick said in my ear. It wasn't a question. A chunk of a nearby pillar launched against the wall closest to our heads. I gasped and tried to pull away, but he yanked back with force on my cock, determined to take me over the edge as the house fell down around us.

"It was all for you." The boy I'd called my best friend, then my lover, then my enemy tugged at my foreskin. He wiggled his finger inside and circled my wet tip. I threw my head back and moaned, not strong enough to fight the pleasure.

"I need you to say you forgive me. Say that you understand why this all had to happen." His demands made me want to escape his grip, but I was close and couldn't stop fucking his hand. Roderick's breath quickened; he was about to shoot too.

"Say it," he said loudly, moisture rolling down his cheek.

"No." As the word came out, I burst between our hands. At the same time, his load shot on his furry stomach.

Directly after we came, Roderick pushed me back with a flat hand on my chest and pointed his finger at my face. "You had a choice to come here. Even when we were kids, you never did know how to turn down a dollar."

Catching my breath, I looked down at the carpet below blanketed with scribbled nonsense and pictures of bearded men. On one sheet was what seemed to be a drawing of the house and grounds. I bent down, grabbing it to rub Roderick's load from my stomach and pubic hair.

While I held it, Roderick scooped the warmth I'd left on him from his abdomen and brought it to his tongue. Swallowing, he seemed angry when he said, "If only one of us makes it out of here, do you think it's going to be you?"

I didn't have a chance to respond before something gave way in the ceiling of Roderick's room and a giant piece of the house fell between the two of us. My first instinct was to make sure he was okay under the piled rubble, but from outside the room a voice yelled, "Alexander, where are you? Hurry!"

CHAPTER FOURTEEN

When I reached the grand foyer again, Darius and Sonny were digging at large chunks of rock pillar that had piled up in front of the French doors.

"It's too high now. You couldn't have gotten here like thirty seconds ago, girl? What were you doing?" Darius said the moment he spotted me. He looked at the cum starting to dry tacky in my fur and my soft cock still flopping in the breeze. "Never mind."

"This is my first earthquake!" Sonny yelled over the constant rumble with some odd excitement in his voice. I didn't have the heart to explain the details I knew, not that I even entirely grasped how or why everything was falling apart around us.

Darius rolled his eyes and grabbed Sonny by the hand. "The wardrobes," he said and led the way up the stairs. Following him, I scraped Roderick's cum from me as quickly as I could and dropped the paper I'd been carrying to the cracking tile.

Shielding our eyes with bent arms above our heads, I didn't know that climbing higher in a crumbling structure was the smartest idea, but we didn't have another choice. The only entrance or exit on the ground floor had always been the back door.

71

My room was the closest to the stairs, but we had to pass by the sitting room to get there. As Darius pulled Sonny and I followed closely behind, he paused our journey abruptly when the antique couch came into view. Inside, the three men turned to one solid structure still sat paralyzed in shades of off-white and gray.

It was a struggle to find the words, but Sonny summed it up perfectly when he gazed upon the statues formed from men he'd been messing around with only days before: "What the fuck?"

Darius picked up the pace immediately, throwing open the door to my room and heading straight to the open closet. While the boys pulled at designer jeans and threw boots across the carpet, I looked to the bathroom, at the purple bathtub now full of wooden planks and cracked building materials. All this luxury was about to be swallowed up by a force I still didn't understand.

A collection of rainbow jockstraps landed on the bed followed by matching tube socks and neoprene harnesses in different configurations. I scooped up one of the only under-garments with a full back and stuffed a leg through a hole, but as Darius and Sonny cleared the panel and started to push toward the cave, it wouldn't budge.

"Help us!" Darius yelled. I let the underwear fall back to the ground. Putting all my weight against the door with the other two men, it didn't move. Behind it, falling rocks against the stone floor echoed. They seemed to be piled up against the access point and filling in the tunnel. This was no longer an exit.

In desperation, Darius grabbed Sonny's hand again and screamed over the constant bangs and thumps, "Let's try mine." From what I knew of the house and its winding passages, Darius's wardrobe was set farther back from the opening to the woods than mine. When I'd brought him through it, we'd passed my wardrobe to get there, but we were out of options.

They moved quickly to the hallway, and I scrambled to keep up, grabbing the underwear I'd been trying to slip into from the carpet on the way. Approaching the door frame after the duo, I ran directly into an unexpected wall. My face smashed against black fabric and more specifically, a breast pocket.

I pulled back to see Usher standing in my way. He walked into the bedroom, pushing me into the caving space and closed the door behind him. "It would end here. In this room," he said and folded his hands in front of him. "This one used to be mine. A long time ago."

"Why are you doing this?" I yelled, tripping backward onto the bed.

Usher laughed and pulled at the hair on his chin. "I wasn't given a rule book, Alexander. I've only done as the house commands. Just like you." His eyes moved to something behind me, and he smiled, only slightly. "Just as I thought," he said.

I turned my head to see the portrait that had spoken to me from the end of the hallway now hanging behind us on an empty wall. Usher continued to speak, and I flipped back to give him my attention.

"I almost asked you to run away with me once. To leave this place and start over, but the house refused to let me go." He put his hands in the pockets of his dress pants and rocked on the heels of his fancy shoes. A piece of plaster from the panel behind him crumbled to dust.

"It only calls to the men who need it most. Like me, you belong here." Usher pointed behind me, and I turned my head again to gaze upon the painting. My facial features were forming on the kneeling man, next to Usher in his suit.

"I'm going to tell you more than I ever knew. For the mansions, the planes, the clothes, wine, everything that comes with this title: You must feed the magic that lives here. You must power the house, or it will turn on you."

Usher walked to a small painting of a man basking nude in ocean waves that had always hung above my nightstand. He traced the face of the older man as if he'd once known him well.

"There's no saying how many men line the grounds of this house and will forever. Sometimes it will feel like you find a new one every day, and some of them, you'll always remember. But you can never feel guilty for being chosen, even if it never stops hurting."

"I don't want any of it anymore. You shouldn't have chosen me." I sat up on the bed. Usher moved in front of me from where he had been gazing at the picture above the nightstand. "We don't have much time now." He shook his head and bit his lip. "There's only one thing I want before the end. I want to finish what we started." The man who had tied me to the house pulled at his tie to loosen the knot and unbuttoned his shirt. With his hairy chest exposed, he leaned in close to where I sat on the bed.

Among the cascade of gear pulled from the wardrobe, I thought about the days and nights I'd longed to dress myself up for him. I remembered all the times I waited for his approval and the craving I developed for his cock and cum inside of me.

"Make it rough," I said, the four-poster bed shaking under me.

Usher smiled before grabbing me by the hair. He tugged hard while I unfastened his belt and released him from his pants. Plaster dust fell on top of us, coating both our hair as our lips made contact. Pushed to my back, I brought my legs above me to offer Usher my hole. I'd cum only moments before and wasn't certain I could again just yet, but I needed to feel him.

With no hesitation, his tip was at the entrance, and I swallowed him inside. His hands around my neck and holding down my hands, I knew I was smiling. We kissed while he stroked me, and when he arched back, something large fell from above us.

CHAPTER FOURTEEN

The portrait jumped from the wall and hit with a crash as Usher shot his load. Soon the house would be rubble.

He withdrew and immediately stripped the rest of his clothes off. Handing over the bundle of his suit, he yelled over the vibration, "There's only one way to stop this now."

I held tight to the clothing as he kissed me one more time. "I did love you, Alexander. Obey the house. The boys will never belong to you. Tighten your heart and—"

The face that had never failed to make me hard and my stomach flutter froze mid-sentence before me. His mustache and beard, the piercing eyes, the fur on his chest. Even his cock, still half-hard from fucking me, was now a provocative nude statue standing in my destroyed quarters.

Posed with one hand on his chest and the other reaching out for me was a man who had never been permitted to truly love another man. I was led to believe he'd possessed everything I could ever want, but it had never been true. According to the House of Otter, this was the kind of man I was destined to become.

Chapter Fifteen

I hadn't noticed the music was still playing until I was gazing upon Usher's powerless form. He'd told us he'd heard the music before, and now I could feel the boys trapped inside the speakers. The violist, the piano player, the dark electronic synth enthusiast—all their talent had been woven into the ambience of the house. This was the choice: be the new leader and give the manor what it wanted or be absorbed. Eaten. Consumed. It seemed we had all been accepted into the structure's lore and would stay part of it one way or another, forever.

Throwing the wrinkled layers of Usher's suit to the carpet, I curved around his stone figure to force open the bedroom door. I looked back only briefly to gaze at the man who had been the source of so much passion and confusion. The only warmth left of him in this world dripped from between my cheeks as I walked away.

In the corridor, everything had been demolished. Sticks of polished furniture splintered with brass tacks and shreds of high thread count fabric lined every inch of the path to Darius's room from mine. I held tight to the walls as they continued to collapse, worried any second the once sturdy floor would give out below me.

When I reached his quarters, I'd hoped to be greeted by nothing at all. I wanted to believe there was a chance Sonny and Darius had found a route through the closet and into the woods. Even if they'd had to leave me behind, I just wanted them to be safe.

But inside, a book lay on the bed, open to drawings of outstretched arms and interlocked hands connecting two men. On one side was Darius in a chef's hat, looking over his shoulder with the bow of an apron resting just above his full ass. On the other page, Sonny was next to a surfboard upright with the ocean behind him, running a hand through his long wavy hair.

Upon seeing the thick black lines, the soundtrack to the mansion's destruction picked up tempo. A beam came loose from above and landed on the bed, splitting the king-sized mattress in two pieces. The thick section of wood was on fire and quickly ignited the canopy and drapes.

I wanted to grab the book, as if I could still save the boys by tucking the collected sketches under my arm. But the blaze spread fast to the pages pinned under the plank. The corners lit and curled until they were dark ash. Their images were gone.

Retreating from the growing inferno, I tried to take the stairs, but the path was blocked by stacked cases full of books, rapidly turning to burning embers. Switching directions, I ran through the sitting room, passed the cemented threesome. It was starting to chip and crack under the weight of the destruction. The looks of pleasure on their faces had turned to fear, as had the men hanging in paintings, pictures, and portraits on the surrounding walls. They were all watching, all begging me to change their fate.

With the bookcase missing, seemingly part of the barricade on the stairs, I was able to access the passage to the kitchen directly. As the house smoldered, the stone below my feet was surprisingly cool. For a moment, in the dark cave, it felt like nothing had changed. Aside from the smell of smoke seeping into my nostrils, I could have been preparing to make a meal and run it up to one of Usher's boys. I could have been sneaking through the passage in cute underwear to entice Usher to put his cock in me. It was then I realized that my former keeper was right: all of this really had been my fault.

Silver trays were spilled everywhere across the tile in the kitchen. Red, white, and rose wine had shattered, leaving puddles of glistening pink between shards of shattered green and transparent glass. I tiptoed carefully but quickly through the mess until I fell through the swinging door to the dining room.

The large table and collection of chairs were back in place, but bits of dried cum from the competitive circle jerk still speckled the shiny hardwood. Candles like the ones from my first dinner with Usher, the one directly before he'd officially made me part of the house, flickered inside the room. It was as if the house had its own strange sense of humor and poetic vengeance. If all the candles throughout the structure had been lit the same way, that explained the fire.

A sudden memory of Roderick and me being pulled by our collars made my knees ache just picturing it. I thought about the way he ignored me until we'd been given permission to touch. He'd followed every rule and had still been punished over and over again by Usher. The only time he'd broken the vows he'd taken was when it involved me. But despite anything he'd said before his load landed on my abdomen, I still wasn't certain if his rule-breaking had all been elaborate sabotage or a way to save me from a worse fate.

Roderick may have never had Usher's love like I did. Even if they'd fucked. Maybe I was trying to convince myself the only reason Usher had slept with the other boys was because he knew he had already broken his vow to the house. That there was no going back so he may as well have some fun. When I emerged in the grand foyer again, something told me I was exactly right. The man I called Usher—but wished I had met as Madden—was still with me. His voice in my head said, "Watch out, boy."

From the side, the Saint Andrew's Cross from the red room barreled in my direction at full force. I dove out of the way, letting my naked body collapse to the punishing tile. The wooden X kept moving until it slammed into the collection of broken house pieces blocking the back entrance to the courtyard. Fire dripped from the impact and what I could still see of the white drapes ignited.

"The pool is caved in. Everything is gone! Where's the suit?" Roderick yelled, pulling the cross-on-wheels back to its starting position. He pushed it again, launching it at the rocks. Even after making contact a second time, nothing moved.

Next to me on the floor, the paper I'd used as a cum rag sat in a scrunchy ball. A word I hadn't noticed before stuck out to me on the drawing of the house: "Front Door."

I pulled at the wad and below something moist and mostly white, but slightly transparent, were the words:

> *Seal the doors.*
> *They will never hurt us where we live again.*
> *I promise.*

I could see him: Madden. A young man who was brought from this house to France. Someone who had grown up in Beachside, just like me. Shoeless feet and worn trunks, he hadn't always been rich like I'd imagined. But, even then, he was incredibly sexy.

The young furry man had gone through everything in almost the same way. Every ritual. But the keeper he'd known as Usher maintained a sweetness about him.

I envisioned a moment in the long history of a manor larger than this one near water people called a sea. In my mind, I saw burning trees and townspeople with lit torches afraid of men who loved other men.

In a ceremony like the one in the dining room, Madden had worn the orange jockstrap and won, but his glory was short lived as his Usher and all the boys inside burned with the house. Their art was transported here, along with a scared young man. Alone and unaware of the rules, he'd created his own and swore he would never let devastation come to the place which had saved his life.

Uncertain if the old one could be rebuilt, Madden's first order as the new Usher had been clear to him the moment he put on his new suit. He had to hide the front door from view and hope no one discriminating in this town would ever discover what went on inside the House of Otter.

/

CHAPTER SIXTEEN

"There's another door!" I yelled to Roderick as he pushed the large wooden cross into the blockage a third time. It hit with a thunderous crash but still, nothing moved. My lungs hurt from inhaling the smoke, and it was getting hard to see.

Roderick ran and grabbed the structure we'd both been restrained to on different occasions. He pulled it back by the riveted straps and yelled, out of breath, "What?"

There wasn't time to explain. I got to my feet and ran to the credenza. Lucky for me, the passage was already open from Roderick retrieving the giant X and wheeling it through. I didn't have to locate the silver button to access the hallway. Even now, it seemed to stretch as long as it always had and glow with the same vibrant red. But this time, it was hot and the illumination came from the roaring blaze.

In the heart of the red room, I gathered everything I could carry, and with armfuls of dildos and butt plugs, whips and sounding rods, I made my way to the spot marked on the forgotten plans. Dropping the collection of toys in a heap in front of the space I called for Roderick, who was still smashing the cross into the rubble.

"Help me!" I yelled and started the excavation by digging a pointed sounding rod across the flat wall opposite the courtyard. In search of a crack in the wallpaper covering it, I knew I'd never seen any indication of a front entrance from the exterior. There was no porch nor steps, no knobs or handles. From the road outside the gate, the architecture had shown nothing but a dark brick wall.

I could see it in my head again, a memory I couldn't be certain the house, or Usher, wanted me to know. Two men close to kissing while a young driver waited for them in the gravel. In a time before I'd come to this place, there had absolutely been a door.

Roderick approached the moment the rod fell into a tight slit. He gasped with amazement and wedged his fingers into the narrow space. I grabbed a whip from the floor, and using the thin but sturdy handle, pried at the opening. When we used our strength together, the plaster began peeling away.

We clawed and smacked the crumbling wall with metal collars and firm double-ended dildos until finally it appeared: a door. The fire had reached the base of the staircase and was edging close to my naked flesh as we cleared the debris and turned the brass knob.

But on the other side, it was as I feared—a brick wall. The flames licked at us, and the beams in the thick pillars continued to collapse. It was over. There was no way out of the house.

Then it appeared, on our island of tile surrounded by a sea of fire: the suit. Usher's suit. Clean, pressed, and hanging next to the gaping hole we'd made in the wall.

"Grab it!" Roderick screamed with desperation. "It's the only way to stop it!" He knew enough for me to believe it was the truth. But I didn't move.

As I hesitated, Roderick said, "Fuck it" and leapt from our oasis into the flames. He grabbed the Saint Andrew's Cross and yelled "Move!" before ramming into the brick wall. The blocks cascaded to the outside and landed on cement with a series of bangs. Roderick's stupid idea had made a space just big enough for a person to crawl through.

"Go!" he screamed, running toward me. I climbed through the space but was stuck until Roderick pushed me through with both hands on my bare ass. Landing on the pavement in a naked heap in front of the house, the first thing I noticed was the sun. I never would have guessed from inside the dark house that outside it was vibrant and beautiful.

The orb shone bright through the trees, highlighting the jagged window we'd dug with hands and sex gear. Peeking through the hole, I reached inside for Roderick but didn't see him. All I saw was fire and melted butt plugs turned to dripping magma.

I yelled for him by name. I yelled that I was sorry. He was gone.

Smoke and flames kissed the blue sky for half my walk back to Beachside. By the time I crossed the tracks, I couldn't even see the ash raining down. It was gathered in my hair though and marked on my body. Even if I could wash it off, I knew then it would always be part of me.

The tourists seemed concerned when I dragged myself straight to the ocean through the hot sand. I'm certain they watched as the dirty naked man with charcoal coated body hair waded in deep enough to float.

There in the ocean, I couldn't hear Usher anymore. I couldn't hear any of them. With my head empty for a moment, I thought about Roderick and how he had sacrificed himself to save me. I'd misjudged him—again. He'd been telling the truth. Everything he'd done really was to help me. To offer me a better life. Roderick offered me the knowledge about the more sinister side of the house as he learned it. He had always wanted me to know.

My cock was hard for some reason. Adrenaline, maybe, I thought. Floating on my back far enough out that I was no longer visible from the sand and with no one nearby, I began to stroke lightly. Figuring if there was anything that could make someone feel alive after nearly meeting their demise, it was a small taste of the little death. The hair of the dog in the form of an orgasm.

Gripping my balls and pinching at my nipple, I thought about the boys first, the friends I was sorry I had ever led, even unintentionally, to the house. I thought about the fun we'd had together the day at the pool, the orgy we'd never completed. My ass puckered thinking about the four men taking turns with each other in the mansion and in our more humble home.

Now I was seeing Usher, but I couldn't make out his face. It was as blurred and fragmented as it had been before we'd met, like the day I'd leaned against the tree and shot my load to the forest floor, imagining him tasting me. I knew there had been more. That at one point, I longed for intimacy with him. He'd been inside of me, kissed me, held me close, but I couldn't remember. My memory of the house seemed to be disappearing as I edged closer to orgasm. All I could see clearly now... was Roderick.

With my cock dripping precum into the salty waves, my fantasy was vivid with the first time we'd ever touched. I could feel the satisfaction of finally swallowing his tongue and cock. In my mind, we pumped at each other in his room, surrounded by files and French language textbooks, and then, I came.

My load shot like I hadn't cum in a thousand years, and that was how long I lay there on the surface of the water once I had. In that state of relaxation, decades could have passed. Days, night, weeks, years with my ears under the small waves, rocking my furry otter body to sleep.

When I finally did open my eyes and swim to shore, it was close to sunset. Oranges, pinks, and yellows lined the horizon I'd never really taken the time to appreciate. This place, this small beach town, really was incredible.

As dusk approached, I spotted two men, probably only a year or so younger than I was, standing together and talking near a bench. My nudity didn't seem to phase them beyond a quick stare and smirk as they passed a business card between them.

"This side says, 'Do you want to make some money?'" One of the young men said, reading the card aloud. He flipped the card over and handed it to the other young man who laughed when he tried to sound out the words then said, "What is this? French? I don't speak French."

The other boy pointed to something on the small paper, "It's in English underneath."

On his second attempt, the boy read it clearly, "His heart is a tightened lute. When one touches it, it echoes."

And I knew then the only man in that house who could have ever lived up to its motto was on his way to France, ready to train his own boys, in his new fancy suit.

THE END

LEO SPARX

Leo Sparx is a digital artist who is bringing his fascination with the history of queer sex to the literary erotica world. Inspiration for his work is often found during virtual orgies, trips to offbeat museums, or classic—occasionally spooky—literature. His unique blend of steamy sensations and dark passion takes the reader on a kinky exploration and allows them to experience encounters in unexpected locations.

www.leosparx.com

instagram.com/authorleosparx

twitter.com/authorleosparx

authorleosparx@gmail.com

More Leo Sparx Books

Before Alexander
Claiming Alexander
Taming Alexander
Saving Alexander

The Case of Armando

4 Horsemen Publications

LGBT Erotica

GRAYSON ACE
How I Got Here
First Year Out of th Closet
You're Only a Top?
You're Only a Bottom?
I Think I'm a Serial Swiper
Lookin in All the Wrong Places

EROTICA

HONEY CUMMINGS
Sleeping with Sasquatch
Cuddling with Chupacabra
Naked with New Jersey Devil
Laying with the Lady in Blue
Wanton Woman in White
Beating it with Bloody Mary

Beau and Professor Bestialora
The Goat's Gruff
Goldie and Her Three Beards
Pied Piper's Pipe
Princess Pea's Bed
Pinnocchio and the Blow Up Doll
Jack's Beanstalk

DALIA LANCE
My Home on Whore Island
Slumming It on Slut Street
Training of the Tramp

72% Match
It was Meant to Be... or Whatever

The Imperfect Perfection

ALI WHIPPE
Office Hours
Tutoring Center
Athletics
Extra Credit

Bound for Release
Fetish Circuit

LGBT FANTASY/PARANORMAL ROMANCE

BLAISE RAMSAY
Through The Black Mirror
The City of Nightmares
The Astral Tower
The Lost Book of the Old Blood
Shadow of the Dark Witch
Chamber of the Dead God

BEAU LAKE
The Beast Beside Me
The Beast Within Me

V.C.WILLIS
The Prince's Priest
The Priest's Assassin
The Assassin's Saint
The Saint's Bloodeater

4HORSEMENPUBLICATIONS.COM